She had a chance now. The two punks would never reach the destination where they planned to kill her. The chase would end in one of two ways. Either the driver would stop and the punks would give themselves up, or there'd be a totaling wreck.

There was no use kidding herself. The driver was not going to stop. But if she died in the inevitable car crash, at least her body would not be found in a Dumpster.

Her two captors had gone silent. She pictured the driver recklessly maneuvering the car, and Hairless looking anxiously out the rear window at the pursuit vehicle.

Hairless broke the silence, but she couldn't quite make out what he was saying.

Though he'd lowered his voice, some of what he was saying came through to her—chilling words that brought back all her previous terror—*"...dump her..."*

Dorothy P. O'Neill

ULTIMATE
DOOM

W🌐RLDWIDE®

TORONTO • NEW YORK • LONDON
AMSTERDAM • PARIS • SYDNEY • HAMBURG
STOCKHOLM • ATHENS • TOKYO • MILAN
MADRID • WARSAW • BUDAPEST • AUCKLAND

Recycling programs
for this product may
not exist in your area.

ULTIMATE DOOM

A Worldwide Mystery/July 2011

First published by Avalon Books

ISBN-13: 978-0-373-26761-3

Printed in U.S.A.

Acknowledgments

With thanks to my writer friends:

Diane Lambright Berry, Nancy Gotter Gates, Helen Goodman, Wendy Greene, Ellen Elizabeth Hunter and Betty DiMeo.

"Dear critics whose verdicts are always so new."
—Henry Austin Dobson
The Ballad of Imitation

PROLOGUE

IN THE OAK-PANELED study of his Park Avenue apartment, Gregory Maybanks maneuvered his oversize body into the leather armchair behind his desk and glared at the letter he'd just removed from its envelope. His fleshy face reddened in anger. With a muttered oath, he turned to the array of buzzers on the adjacent wall and jabbed the one connected to his wife's bedroom.

He knew Thelma would be there. He'd glimpsed her only a few minutes ago when he arrived home from his office. She'd been fleeing down the corridor toward the bedroom wing, pretending she hadn't heard the elevator door open or Oleg's customary, "Good evening, sir."

He had no doubt Thelma knew about this letter. She'd seen Oleg bring in the mail and place it on his desk. He pictured her in his study, going through the mail, trembling at the sight of the envelope bearing the name of the private day school Emily attended. She knew it was another letter from the headmistress, informing him of their daughter's latest scholastic or behavioral problem. Thelma knew he was right in blaming her for this. She'd failed to do her part in creating a home environment necessary for the proper development of Emily's mind and character.

Again, he scowled at the letter. The D average and being caught cheating on an exam were bad enough, but now Emily had started talking back to her teachers. "Insolence and disrespect," the headmistress called it. She hadn't threatened expulsion yet. He'd do everything possible to keep that from happening. Having his children in prestigious schools was important to his image as one of Manhattan's leading citizens.

Entrusting Thelma with the upbringing of their daughter had been a mistake. He'd believed she'd be as capable as he for the job of becoming a middle-aged parent and helping him prove his theory that environment was the key factor in the development of a child's character and intellect. He wouldn't have married her if he hadn't believed she'd have as much success with a daughter as he would with a son.

The thought of their son dispelled some of his anger. Kevin was proof positive that his belief in the power of environment wasn't just some crackpot idea. Kevin was a boy any father would be proud of. High scholastic achievement, athletic skills, winning personality—he had it all. Also, unlike many kids his age, Kevin never dressed like a freak. He liked tweed jackets, well-tailored khaki slacks and clean white t-shirts or button-downs. Now in his last year of prep at Choate, he'd been accepted at Princeton. He'd have been a shoo-in even if his old man weren't an alumnus and hadn't endowed a new academics building.

After college there'd be a job waiting for Kevin at Maybanks Enterprises. Together, they'd continue the strategies that had made Gregory Maybanks a billionaire. As Maybanks & Son, they'd change the skyline of Manhattan.

With Kevin, he'd succeeded almost beyond his expectations.

His feeling of triumph faded as he thought, again, of Thelma's failure. Emily was thirteen now, and showed signs of being pretty, but she was developing into an airhead. There was no excuse for this. Emily had been raised in the same cultured, privileged environment as Kevin. If Thelma had done her job right…

What the devil was keeping her? He jabbed at the buzzer again.

IN THE BATHROOM ADJOINING her bedroom, Thelma Maybanks dabbed cold water on her eyes. She still had enough pride to pull herself together before answering the summons to Gregory's study. She ran a comb through her hair, trying to ignore the graying blond strands and outdated hairdo.

She could have gone to New York's most sought after hairdresser and rubbed elbows with the likes of Elizabeth Taylor and Hillary Clinton. Gregory was no penny-pincher. His one redeeming trait. He wouldn't have cared how much money she spent on herself. Not because he'd ever loved her, but because he wanted Mrs. Gregory Maybanks to reflect his success. He maintained accounts for her at all the upscale shops. And, like her expensive clothes, she knew the Christmas furs, diamonds and other luxury items were part of an image he wanted to maintain. But at least his hypocrisy didn't include their wedding anniversary. He'd never made much of it. By the time he stopped remembering she barely remembered it herself.

She couldn't recall when she'd stopped caring about her appearance. She knew she'd never been a beauty, but even at age thirty-nine, twenty years ago, she'd caught the eye of rising real estate tycoon, Gregory Maybanks, when he came into the law office where she worked as a file clerk. Now he rarely looked at her at all, except when he was raging at her about Emily.

When the buzzer sounded again, she longed to rip it out of the wall, hurl it to the floor and stomp on it. Twenty—even ten years ago, she would have. But two decades of marriage to Gregory Maybanks had sapped all the spunk out of her.

She'd done the best she could with Emily, but it became apparent to her that the best environment in the world wasn't going to work with Emily as it had with Kevin. Refusing to admit that his belief in the power of environment might be flawed, Gregory blamed *her*. His tirades of bitter recrimination became a daily occurrence, crushing her spirit until she found herself without the will or the courage to stand up to him.

More than once, before her spirit had been completely quelled, she'd contemplated divorce. But Gregory and his attorneys would have made sure there'd be as small a settlement as possible. Because she was the one who wanted out, it could have been nothing. She had no money of her own for an attorney, no family to help tide her over until she could find a job.

And the children. Gregory would have demanded and received full custody. Kevin would have been all right. To Gregory, Kevin was living proof that his theory was indisputable. But Emily represented failure. What would become of her if she were left to cope with Gregory, alone?

With a deep sigh, she turned toward the door. She'd better get to the study before the buzzer sounded a third time. He'd be angry enough, having to call her twice. She should be thankful his anger was confined to words, but sometimes she thought being physically abused would be no worse than the verbal blows that left her spirit bruised beyond healing.

In the hall, she paused at the door to Emily's room, kept closed to confine her calico cat, Patches. Emily hadn't come home from school yet. The school van should have dropped her off almost two hours ago, but she hadn't called out, "I'm home, Mom!" as she always did. Maybe Emily had slipped into her room without her usual greeting. Thelma wanted to knock on the door, but she knew she must not delay any longer in getting to the study.

If Emily knew about the letter from her school, she might have put off a confrontation with her father by not coming inside when the school van dropped her off. She'd done this before. She'd gone for a walk or stopped in to visit a friend in the building. Thelma pictured a dejected Emily, dreading the moment when she must face her father's wrath.

Emily had been a sweet baby. She would have grown into a happy young girl if Gregory hadn't wrung all the joy out of her, starting in kindergarten, when it became apparent she was a slow learner. But she was still young enough to have some spirit left. Sooner or later she'd reach the boiling point and rebel against his constant tongue lashings. Thelma didn't even want to imagine Gregory's reaction when this happened.

Just as she reached the front hall, she saw Kevin getting off the elevator. Tall, dark haired, handsome and debonair, as always, he wore the Irish tweed hacking jacket Gregory had given him for his birthday. It cost more than many wage earners earned in a month. No sloppy teen attire for Kevin. He liked to dress well, and he knew how to maintain a look of classic affluence without crossing the line and becoming the butt of peer derision.

He'd come home from school, unexpectedly, for the weekend. Good, Thelma thought. Gregory was always in a better mood when Kevin was around.

"Kevin, dear," she said. "This is a nice surprise."

His face broke into a broad smile. He caught her up in a big hug, saying, "Hi, Mom."

What a winning way he had. He could charm the birds off the trees—even a mean old buzzard like his father, she thought, with a wry smile. *At least Gregory couldn't control what she was thinking.*

"Are you going to be home all weekend?" she asked.

"Yeah—till Sunday afternoon." He glanced toward the study. "Dad home yet?"

"Yes. He just buzzed for me and I was on my way. Come with me." He'd be a buffer, she thought.

She was right. When they entered the study Gregory sprang to his feet, the expression on his face faintly reminiscent of the way he'd looked when they'd first met, more than twenty years ago. Then forty, Gregory Maybanks had been a good-looking man with a compelling personality.

The good looks were long gone. The compelling personality remained, but it was dominated by the driving force he'd acquired over the years—the theory which became his ruling passion from the moment he knew they were to be parents.

Just two others knew about Gregory's theory and his overwhelming need to prove it. They were his only real friends: Elliott Ray and Conrad Schuler. She knew they didn't agree with his idea. She'd overheard the three of them arguing about it more than once. But they had to admit it seemed to be working with Kevin.

According to Gregory's plan, in early infancy both children had been given plenty of attention and surrounded by expensive, educational toys. When Emily was a newborn, it was already obvious that Kevin was the proof in his father's pudding. From then on, Kevin's wish was his father's command. Now, at eighteen, his personal spending money exceeded the minimum wage. He had carte blanche at every upscale establishment in Manhattan. He was given a Corvette for his birthday.

But poor, dear Emily—her development had disappointed Gregory early on. She was almost two before she began to say the usual baby words, and she didn't really talk until she was well beyond three. By the time she reached kindergarten age she hadn't shown any interest in her carefully selected books and educational toys, preferring to play with stuffed animals instead. Now, at thirteen, she was a mediocre student.

Physicians told Gregory not to be concerned. "I see many children like Emily," one pediatrician said. "She'll get along okay." But this did not satisfy Gregory.

If Kevin had not started talking when he was barely a year old—if he had not shown interest in letters and numbers before he was three—if, by the time he was in kindergarten, he hadn't been reading at first grade level, perhaps Emily's slow development wouldn't have been as noticeable.

She watched father and son embrace. "Sit down, son, and tell me what's been going on at Choate," Gregory said.

Quietly, Thelma left the study, knowing he was too absorbed with Kevin to notice. His anger with her and with Emily had been submerged, but it was still there, smoldering beneath his feelings for his son. Deep feelings of pride, affection and perhaps most of all, triumph.

She encountered Bruna in the hall. Bruna and her husband, Oleg, had worked in the household for more than seven years. Gregory's overbearing manner had driven away a parade of maids, cooks and butlers over the years, but Oleg and Bruna had settled into the servants' quarters with Ukrainian stoicism. The only other servant at present was Mariette, a young Haitian woman who came in daily to assist Bruna.

"Emily, she come home, Madam," Bruna said in her thick Slavic accent. "She gone to her room."

"Thank you, Bruna." Thelma went directly to Emily's door and knocked.

Emily's voice sounded cross. "Who's there?"

"It's Mother. May I come in, dear?"

Emily opened the door. She was holding her beloved Patches in her arms. She'd always been a thin child. Now the frightened, unhappy expression on her face added a look of pathetic frailty.

"The school sent Father a letter," she said.

"Yes, I know," Thelma replied. "I guess your father read it, but I haven't seen it yet." She sat down on a flowered chintz chaise among an assortment of teddy bears. "What happened, dear?"

"I hate school," Emily said. "I feel so dumb. I can't keep up with the other kids and the teachers are always picking on me."

"Your teachers are only trying to help you."

"No, they're not. I told all of them to quit hassling me."

"Oh, Emily—that sounds as if you were rude to them."

Emily bit at her lip. "I guess I was."

"Is that what the letter was about?"

"That and me not apologizing."

"When you go to school on Monday you can tell your

teachers you're sorry you were discourteous. Then I'm sure everything will be all right."

A spark of defiance flashed in Emily's eyes. "I'm never going to apologize."

"Your father will insist on it."

"He can't make me. I hope I get expelled."

She *wants* to be expelled, Thelma thought. She shuddered, thinking of Gregory's reaction. "You know your father won't stand for this. He'll take you over to your school, and…"

"I won't go with him!" Emily said with such vehemence that Patches broke out of her arms and scurried under the bed. "I'll run away. I hate school. I hate Father."

Thelma sighed, not as much about Emily's outburst concerning her father, but more for wishing she had the courage to say it herself.

Maybe if she changed the subject, Emily would cool down. "Here's something to cheer you up. Kevin's home for the weekend."

Emily brightened. She and her brother had always been close. "Kevin's here? Is he in his room? I want to talk to him about something."

"He's with your father. Is this something you could talk to me about?"

"I wanted to ask him if he could persuade Father to let me go to a public school. Mariette says her brother's in public school and getting along fine and he can't even speak English very well."

Apparently Emily had told Mariette all about her

problems at school. Thelma felt thankful Gregory didn't know about this. One more reason to rant at her, saying she was so inadequate as a mother that their daughter chose to confide in the Haitian maid.

"I doubt if your father would consider putting you in a public school, dear," she said. What an understatement, she thought. Like his wife's expensive clothes, jewelry and sable coat, Gregory Maybanks's daughter must attend a prestigious private school. Anything less would mar his precious image.

She rose from the chaise. "Dinner will be soon. But don't worry about your father scolding you at the table. With your brother home, he'll be in a good humor—at least while we're eating."

She hoped the good humor would last until Sunday afternoon, when Kevin's Corvette would roar out of the underground parking garage and head north on Park Avenue en route to Connecticut. After that, the ordeal of living with Gregory Maybanks would resume.

Long ago she'd resigned herself to enduring it, and Emily had accepted it with meek forbearance. But now, the defiance she'd glimpsed in Emily's eyes and the hatred she'd heard in her voice told her that her sweet, mild-mannered daughter was on the verge of rebellion. She sighed, wishing she, too, had the spirit to rebel, and the next time Gregory buzzed her into his study to rant at her, she could tell him to drop dead.

ONE

Liz Rooney was getting ready to turn in for the night when her phone rang. She glanced at the clock on the wall opposite the sofa bed. Five minutes past eleven. Who'd be calling her at this hour?

She checked the caller ID and saw the name of her boss, Medical Examiner Dan Switzer. She answered. "Dan—what's up?"

"Lizzie—I just got word of a homicide. I'm going out on this one. If you want to go along, I'll pick you up in about twenty minutes."

His words were barely spoken before she started getting out of her pajamas. "Sure, I want to go with you, Dan. I'll meet you in front of my building."

Dan knew she was always up for going to the scene of a homicide, she thought, throwing on a shirt and slacks and grabbing her blue wool blazer. He and her father were long time friends. They'd been encouraging her passion for following murder cases since she was a teenager and Pop was a NYPD Homicide detective. She wished Pop hadn't retired from the force. He and Mom lived in Florida now. Besides missing them both, she missed Pop's knowledgeable input.

When Dan retired, it wouldn't be so easy to follow

homicides and match wits with detectives. It wasn't likely that any other Medical Examiner would allow her to go to murder scenes with him or let her in on forensic information. There'd be a huge void in her life without the challenge of trying to figure things out, the excitement of stumbling on an important clue and the satisfaction of knowing she'd helped solve a case.

But the future of her hobby was by no means hopeless. After months of hostility, she and Homicide Detective George Eichle had finally buried the hatchet. His negative attitude toward her interest in murder cases had mellowed after she'd turned up some important clues for him in recent homicide cases. He'd started to let her in on developments ahead of the media. Three days ago they'd agreed to be friends and they'd started calling one another Liz and Ike, instead of Rooney and Eichle. But would he ever become her main source of information?

She picked up her purse, put on her blazer and headed for the door. Dan hadn't mentioned where the murder had taken place. She hoped it had happened in Ike's precinct and that he'd be sent out on it. *Ike.* She wasn't used to thinking of Detective Eichle that way. If she ran into him tonight, it would be their first encounter at a crime scene as friends instead of adversaries.

It would be strange not to have him glare at her in frank hostility and ask, "What are you doing here, Rooney?" But she knew his disapproval of her presence at homicide scenes was over with, along with their frequent verbal clashes. But he probably wouldn't stop teasing her about her Irish redhead's temper.

What a difference a few weeks could make, she thought, as she locked her apartment door and started down the stairs. Months ago, she and her best friend, Sophie Pulaski, had agreed that Detective George Eichle was a grouch. Sophie was a rookie cop in Ike's precinct—a feisty little blonde who wanted to be a Homicide detective. They'd called Ike Detective Pickle Puss behind his back.

Now she thought of Ike as a nice guy with a good sense of humor, and not bad looking, either. The first time she'd met him, years ago when Pop brought her, a hooked-on-homicides teenager, into the station house, she'd formed an impression of a tall young man with a shock of sandy hair. It wasn't until recently that she'd noticed he had hazel eyes.

She hadn't told Sophie, yet, that Detective Pickle Puss had become Ike. Sophie would immediately decide this new friendship was the beginning of something more. Since Sophie got engaged to be married she wanted everyone else to fall in love, too.

In the lower hall, she tiptoed past the Moscarettis' apartment door. Friendly building owners Rosa and Joe Moscaretti were also the superintendents. From the first day she moved into the nineteenth century house Joe and Rosa had remodeled into four apartments, they'd appointed themselves *her* superintendents. "A nice girl living alone in New York can't be too careful," Rosa had said.

If they heard her going out at this late hour, she'd have some explaining to do.

In the car, Dan told her where they were headed. A swanky, Park Avenue address. This sounded like a case involving someone wealthy and important, Liz thought.

"Do you have any details?" she asked.

"The murder victim is Gregory Maybanks," he replied.

"The real estate tycoon?" She'd heard about him in news reports. He owned property all over Manhattan and had put up several large buildings, including two skyscrapers.

"That's the one. The cop who called me said a servant found him dead at his desk tonight, shortly after half-past-ten. He'd been struck on the head with a heavy object."

"Who phoned the police?"

"His wife."

Like everyone in New York who kept up with the news, Liz knew that billionaire real estate tycoon Gregory Maybanks lived with his wife and a son and daughter in one of the posh residential towers he'd put up during the past ten or fifteen years.

ENTERING THE LOBBY OF the Maybankses' apartment building, Liz took careful notice of the layout. She'd followed enough homicide cases to know this scrutiny helped clip the wings of her often flyaway imagination. For example—the security guard's station faced a bank of elevators. In addition to being signed in and out, no one could get on or off an elevator without being seen by the guard. The fire stairway, situated near the elevators, and the door to the underground-parking garage were also in full view of the security station.

The guard directed them to a private elevator. The Maybanks apartment was on the eighth floor. It probably overlooked the gardenlike mall in the center of Park Avenue, Liz thought.

They stepped off the elevator into a foyer. Liz saw a living room on the left, and glimpsed part of a dining room. She had an overall impression of Oriental rugs, rich velours and damasks and gleaming mahogany. And spaciousness. This apartment must take up the entire eighth floor, she decided.

A uniformed cop greeted them. "The body's in there, Dr. Switzer," he said, motioning toward an open doorway to the right. "Your crew got here a few minutes ago. The detectives are here, too. They've taken photos."

Through the doorway, Liz saw a cluster of people at the scene. One of them was Ike's partner, Lou Sanchez. That meant Ike was on the case, too. They entered the room. Paneled walls and floor-to-ceiling bookshelves. Maybanks's study.

Gregory Maybanks was slumped in a leather armchair at his desk, his face buried in a mass of scattered papers. The thinning hair on top of his head was matted with congealed blood.

"Looks like his heart stopped pumping soon after he was struck," one of the forensic crew told Dan.

The murder weapon had to be something like a brass

candlestick or a fireplace poker, Liz thought. But there was no fireplace in the study, no mantel where a brass candle stick might have stood.

While Dan prepared to examine the body, she looked around for Ike. Just as she decided he was interviewing family members or servants, a familiar voice came from behind her.

"What are you doing here, Rooney?"

Hearing him ask the detested question and call her Rooney again was like being dealt two physical blows. She turned around, bracing herself for the glowering look she'd hoped she'd never see again.

"I'm kidding, Liz," he said. His smile was like balm on a sore spot.

"Very funny," she replied, but she spoke lightly and with an answering smile. She didn't want him telling her to hold on to her redhead temper.

"I didn't expect to see you here. I thought Dan might decide you'd gone to bed," he said.

"Dan knows I'd always wake up for a crime scene." She glanced at the body. "Any ideas yet?"

He shook his head. "It's too soon. We've finished interviewing the two servants, but we've only spoken briefly to the family members. We want to do a more thorough interview with them after we hear what the Medical Examiner has to say."

"Has the apartment been searched for evidence yet?" she asked. She wondered if the murder weapon had been found and what it might be.

"The uniforms are going over the kitchen and servants' quarters now. They'll be ready to search the family bedrooms after that."

Liz glanced around the study, looking for family members.

Ike must have noticed the glance. "The wife and son were in the study with the two servants when we arrived. They've gone to their bedrooms."

"There's a daughter, too, isn't there?"

"Right. Mrs. Maybanks said the daughter has been asleep and doesn't know what happened. I told Mrs. Maybanks to let her sleep till we're ready to question the family." He cast her a grin. "You're doing some questioning yourself."

"Sorry. I know you don't have time to fill me in now."

"Right. Not now. I see Lou signaling me."

She watched him leave the study with his partner. His attitude was a far cry from previous murder scene encounters. He'd tell her how the questioning went. In the meantime, while she waited for Dan, she'd find a place to sit down and write some observations in her notebook.

She seated herself in a chair near the doorway and looked around the room at the handsome furnishings— walls hung with what were probably rare, old prints, bookshelves filled with leather-bound volumes. A section of wall near her chair contained photographs. One was in color, unmistakably a family group.

She studied the photo and decided it was a fairly recent shot of Gregory Maybanks and his family. The father figure in the picture had the same corpulent body as the man slumped, lifeless, at his desk across the room. The slender, blonde mother might have been attractive if it weren't for the tense look on her face. The daughter looked about twelve, maybe thirteen. She was thin and rather frail looking and had reddish-blond hair. The son, probably sixteen or seventeen, was dark haired and very handsome.

Next to the family photo she noticed several black and white photos of three young men together. She got the feeling they were close friends. Even if one of the photos hadn't shown them standing around a big car with flaring fins, she would have known by their clothes and hair that the pictures were old. One of the boys looked vaguely like Gregory Maybanks, she thought. He'd piled on a few pounds since then. The photos were probably taken in his college days. He must still be friends with the two others to have kept the photos all these years and displayed them in his study.

She scanned the room for more details. On a wall close to the desk, she saw a row of buzzer buttons—six of them. One for the kitchen. One for each servant's room. They must have a lot of servants, she decided. Curious, she got up and walked over to have a look.

Each button was labeled. As she expected, one said *Kitchen.* Two said *Servant #1* and *Servant #2.* But the other three said *Kevin, Emily* and *Mrs. M.*

She stared at them in disbelief. What kind of man would sit in his study and summon his family by buzzer? Especially his wife. A real jerk would, she decided, turning away from the buzzers in disgust.

There were too many people gathered around the body for her to get a good look at the objects on the desk, but she managed to see something that looked like a small, bronze, winged dragon near some overturned books. A bookend. Where was the other one? Was the missing bookend the murder weapon? Had the killer taken it, or had it been bagged as evidence? She jotted her observations in her notebook.

She didn't see any signs of a possible robbery. She wished she'd asked Ike if the deceased's wallet had been stolen.

The study had French doors along the outside wall. That meant there was a balcony overlooking Park Avenue. When she and Dan pulled up in front of the building, it was too dark to see if there were other balconies. If there were, could an agile perpetrator have gained access to the study from another apartment? She wished the French doors weren't closed, so she could look outside. She'd learned to sit on her hands at murder scenes. Nothing must be touched, including doorknobs. No doubt the doors were locked at night, but today's weather was mild. Gregory Maybanks might have opened them during the evening while he was in his study. The killer could have come in that way and closed the doors when making a getaway. She wished the doors were open now. It was getting uncomfortably warm in the study. She went back to her chair, took off her blazer and hung it over the arm.

Dan showed no signs of finishing up. She glanced out into the hallway. Cops were all over the place. It looked as if they'd finished searching the kitchen and servants' quarters. Maybe they'd have some information.

Just as she walked over to two cops standing near the elevator, a middle-aged woman approached from a corridor. The hem of a pink nightgown protruded below her green-and-tan plaid bathrobe, almost down to her pink crocheted bedroom booties. Her dark brown, gray flecked hair hung in one long, fat braid down her back.

Her sweeping glance included all the cops and Liz. "You want it coffee?" she asked. "I got coffee in kitchen. Tea, too."

The cops looked regretful. "Thanks, ma'am," one replied. "But we need to stay out here till we get the go ahead to search the other bedrooms."

The woman nodded. "Is okay. I gonna be bring."

As she turned to go, Liz hastened to her side. "I'll help you bring the coffee out," she said. "And then I'd love to have a cup of tea in the kitchen."

"You not a police?" the woman asked.

"No, I'm here with the Medical Examiner."

Again, the woman nodded. "You gonna be come with me."

Liz followed her along the corridor to the gleaming white tile and stainless steel kitchen. An aroma rich enough to start all the cops salivating came from an over-size coffeemaker. On a table stood a china tea service.

"We gonna be use paper cups for police," the woman said, stacking a bunch of them on a tray. She added a bowl of sugar, a pitcher of milk and some spoons. "You carry pot, I carry tray," she said.

They put everything on a table near the elevator. When they started back to the kitchen, Liz looked over her shoulder. The cops were going for the coffee like a herd of trail-parched cattle at a waterhole.

"You were very thoughtful to make coffee," she said, as they entered the kitchen. She thrust out her hand. "My name is Liz Rooney."

The woman clasped the offered hand. "Bruna Lenko," she replied. "My husband and me, we keep house." She glanced toward a hallway off the kitchen.

"My husband, he rest now. He got it terrible shock. He find the boss dead."

"It must have been awful for him," Liz said. "And I know it was a shock for everyone. How's the family doing?"

"Madam—she doing pretty good. She in her room. I gonna be take it tea for her soon." She picked up the teapot. "You sit," she said, pouring tea into two cups.

Here was her chance to get some information, Liz thought. Ike had already interviewed the servants. He'd intimated that he'd let her know how the questionings went, but that didn't mean he'd tell her everything. She wanted to find things out for herself.

"How are the children?" she asked.

"Kevin—he big boy but he cry like baby. He in his room. The police talking to him now."

"How about the daughter?"

"Emily—she sleep. She not know what happen. Madam, she gonna be wake her up for talk to cops."

"Were the children close to their father?"

Bruna gave a blank stare. "Close?"

"Did they have a loving relationship?"

"Loving," Bruna repeated. "Kevin and the boss okay but Emily…" She shook her head. "With Emily the boss all the time *zloy.*"

Zloy. Liz decided that meant angry. Bruna's next words proved her right.

"Emily, she not do good in school. The boss, he all the time yell at her why she not do good like Kevin."

"That must have been hard on Emily, being scolded all the time."

Bruna nodded. "Most times, Emily, she just cry and not say nothing when he yell, but tonight she yell back at him. They got it big fight after dinner. The boss, he say he gonna be punish her."

"Punish her? How?"

"He say he gonna be take her cat to animal place for kill. He know Emily, she love her cat. Emily, she call him bad name and run to her mother room."

Liz's senses went on alert. This was more information than she'd expected. Gregory Maybanks was coming across as a mean man and Emily as a mild-mannered girl who'd reached the breaking point.

"Where were Emily and her father when this happened?" she asked.

"In hall by door to boss study room."

"Do you remember how long after dinner this was, or what time it was?"

"Yes. It happen few minutes after everyone leave table. I see Madam and Kevin go to their rooms, but

Emily, she in hall with the boss. I hear clock strike seven. Then I hear yelling. Then, Emily, she run down hall and I hear her calling mother. The boss, he go in his study room and slam door. Nobody see him again till my husband find him, dead."

Something about the way Bruna described Gregory Maybanks's actions motivated Liz's next question. "Did you like the boss?"

Bruna gave her a long look before replying. "The boss, he not much to like. He nice only to Kevin." She drained her teacup and got to her feet. "I gonna be take it tea to Madam now."

"And I should be getting back to the study," Liz said. "Thanks for the tea, Bruna."

So, Maybanks wasn't nice to the servants, his daughter or his wife, Liz thought, as she left the kitchen and walked down the corridor. As Bruna had put it, he wasn't much to like. This didn't surprise her. She already knew he used a buzzer to summon his wife when he wanted to talk to her, and he wouldn't hesitate to break his daughter's heart by having her beloved cat put to sleep because she was doing poorly in school.

Just as she got to the front hall, she heard what sounded like someone knocking loudly on a door. The noise was coming from the hall opposite the elevator—the bedroom wing, she decided. She heard a door open and an agitated male voice.

"Mom, what's the matter? I'm talking to the detectives. Can't this wait?"

A woman's voice rose, shrill, almost hysterical. "No,

it can't wait, Kevin. I just went to wake up Emily so she'd be ready to talk to the detectives, and she's not in her room and her bed hasn't been slept in. She's gone, and her cat's gone, too. I'm afraid she's taken Patches and run away."

TWO

LIZ HEARD KEVIN MAYBANKS try to calm his mother. "Oh, come on, Mom, she wouldn't run away. This isn't the first time Dad's chewed her out."

Mrs. Maybanks's voice was choked with tears. "He never threatened to take Patches away from her before."

Liz heard Ike's voice. "Let's have a look around the apartment. Maybe Emily went to the kitchen for a snack and took her cat along for a saucer of milk."

But they'd all seen Emily's bed undisturbed, Liz thought.

Ike knew she'd left the apartment sometime during the evening, instead of going to sleep. He was being kind, trying to calm Mrs. Maybanks.

At that moment, Bruna entered the corridor with a tea tray. She looked surprised to see Liz there.

"Emily's missing," Liz explained. "I heard Mrs. Maybanks tell Kevin she wasn't in her room when she went to wake her up."

Bruna stared at her for a moment. "You bring," she said, handing the tea tray to Liz. "I gonna be go to Madam, quick." She hurried toward the bedrooms.

This was her chance to see Mrs. Maybanks and

Kevin, Liz decided. She brushed away the thought of Ike's reaction when she appeared.

They were all in one of the bedrooms. Emily's bedroom, she decided. Lots of flowered chintz and an array of stuffed animals on the bed. Bruna had her arms around a sobbing woman in a blue robe. Mrs. Maybanks. If it weren't for her disheveled, graying blond hair and tear-stained face, she might have been somewhat pretty. The good-looking young man, wearing a tartan plaid bathrobe over pajamas, had to be Kevin. He, too, was trying to comfort his mother.

Through an open door, she saw Emily's bathroom with the cat's litter box and feeding dishes arranged on the floor on opposite sides of a pedestal sink. Ike and Lou, interrupted in their questioning of Kevin, were in there, conferring about this latest development.

She set the tea tray down on the dresser. Ike came into the bedroom at that moment and saw her. She hoped she was only imagining a trace of "What are you doing here, Rooney?" in his eyes.

"Bruna made tea for Mrs. Maybanks and asked me to bring it to her," she explained.

The explanation seemed to satisfy Ike. "Sit down and have a cup of tea, Mrs. Maybanks," he said. "It will do you good."

He had a warm, kind way about him, she thought. She couldn't imagine him being gruff or hard-hearted, like detectives on TV cop shows. But she could never picture Pop being that way, either, although he'd told her he often had to be.

Mrs. Maybanks cast Ike an appreciative look. She sat down on a chaise. Liz brought the tray to her.

"Thank you," Mrs. Maybanks said. "Are you one of the detectives?"

To tell her she was with the Medical Examiner would only distress her further, Liz thought. It would remind her that her husband's murdered body was still in his study.

How should she reply? Before she could decide, Ike spoke up. "Ms. Rooney is part of the investigation."

She had only an instant to smile her thanks at him. She caught his fleeting glance and the suggestion of a grin before he abruptly addressed Bruna.

"You say Emily hasn't been in the kitchen?"

"No. I not see her since she run to Madam room after dinner."

"Emily's brother told us there was an argument between her and her father after dinner. Do you know anything about that?"

Bruna nodded. "Big fight."

"You didn't mention that when I interviewed you earlier."

"You not ask me nothing about fight," Bruna retorted. Liz had to smile. Bruna was not someone to be intimidated.

"Emily wouldn't run away because of an argument with Dad," Kevin said. "She's probably in the building, somewhere. Maybe she went to see that friend of hers, Susan. You know she's gone there before with Patches, Mom."

"Susan and her parents are out of town for the weekend," Mrs. Maybanks said. She began to weep.

"Please don't cry, Mom," Kevin said. "If she's not visiting Susan, she's visiting one of her friends in the neighborhood. She couldn't have run away. Where would she go? Do you know if she had any money?"

"Only what she might have saved from her last allowance," Mrs. Maybanks replied. Tears rolled down her face. "Oh, my poor baby. What's going to happen to her, wandering around the city at night?"

Liz thought Mrs. Maybanks seemed terribly distraught over her daughter's disappearance, but Bruna had said she was taking her husband's death calmly.

"She couldn't have gone far, holding the cat," Ike said.

"Oh, she has a cat carrier for taking Patches to the vet," Kevin said. "If she was going any distance, maybe she took it." He opened a cabinet door, adding, "She keeps her cat stuff in here."

Liz caught sight of a basket of cat toys on a shelf, along with some large bags of cat food and litter, before Kevin turned around, his face stricken with worry.

"The carrier's gone," he said.

"I knew it—she's run away," Mrs. Maybanks cried out. Ike must be gritting his teeth in aggravation, Liz thought.

Here he was, investigating a homicide, and he'd barely started interviewing before he was into a missing persons case.

She saw him muttering something to Lou. Probably

something about calling the security guard to find out if Emily had left the building this evening, what time and what she was wearing. Emily's disappearance had really put the brakes on the investigation. At this rate, it would be morning before Ike and Lou got statements from everyone in the household.

Just then a cop appeared in the doorway, saying the Medical Examiner was finished. He asked whether the family wanted to see the deceased before he was taken for autopsy.

"No, thank you," Mrs. Maybanks said. Kevin shook his head. "I'll pass, too."

One look at the battered, lifeless body had been enough for them, Liz decided.

As the cop turned away, Liz asked if he'd tell Dan she'd be ready to leave with him in a minute.

"I'm going now," she told Ike. "I hope you can finish up in time for breakfast."

"We'll manage," Ike said. "So long, Liz. I'll get back to you tomorrow."

Liz said goodbye to Mrs. Maybanks, who smiled through her tears. "Thank you for being so kind," she said. "Everyone has been so kind."

As Liz left the bedroom, she heard Kevin's voice. "Detective Eichle, the officers could be searching my bedroom while we're all in here." A perceptive young man, she thought. He realized his sister's disappearance was holding up the investigation.

On the elevator with Dan, she was struck with an idea.

She could question the security guard and find out if Emily or anyone else from the Maybankses' apartment had left the building tonight. She could phone the information to Ike from the lobby. This was one less detail Ike and Lou would have to attend to. It would save them a few minutes.

When they got off the elevator, she turned to Dan.

"Would you mind if I spoke to the security guard? I'll make it quick."

He gave an indulgent smile. "Sure—go ahead. I'll wait for you at the entrance."

The guard, a lanky, balding, black man, looked up with a smile when she approached his desk.

"What can I do for you, young lady?" He'd just seen her get off the Maybankses' private elevator. He knew she must have some connection to the case.

"Were you on duty earlier in the evening?" she asked.

"No, miss. I came on at midnight."

"Did the other guard leave a record of who entered and left the building tonight?" she asked.

"Yes, miss…" He opened a drawer. "Terrible, what happened up there," he said. "I couldn't believe it. This building is one of the most secure in the city."

He brought out a clipboard and scanned it. "Here it is. Emily Maybanks left the building at ten minutes to nine."

"Did anyone else enter the Maybankses' apartment or leave it tonight?"

He scanned the records again. "Nobody came in since the girl at quarter-of-five and the boy at ten-of-six, and nobody left except the maid, Mariette Fournier, at six-twelve, until the girl left at ten-to-nine."

"Thanks," Liz said. "May I use your phone to call the Maybankses' apartment?"

"Of course." Ike must have been standing within arm's reach of a phone. Maybe he was intercepting all calls. Anyway, he picked up on the first ring.

"Ike—it's me, Liz. I'm in the lobby. I just talked to the security guard and…"

"You found out Emily left the building and the time." He didn't sound surprised.

"Yes. It was ten-minutes-to-nine. And the only other person from the Maybankses' apartment who left the building tonight was the maid at ten-after-six."

"Thanks, Liz. You saved us some time." His voice took on a teasing tone. "Did you tell the guard you were a cop?"

"Don't you think I know where to draw the line?"

"I'm never quite sure. But, nice work, Liz."

"I wish I could have found out what Emily was wearing, but there's a different guard on now."

"We have that covered. Bruna and Mrs. Maybanks went through Emily's closet and couldn't find her pink jacket. We figure that's what she had on when she left."

He was being very patient, she thought, as she hung up the phone. He must be itching to get through with the interviews.

IN THE CAR, Dan told her that Gregory Maybanks hadn't been dead more than two or three hours when they arrived at the scene.

"Looks like he was struck twice and died within minutes," he said.

"I saw one bronze, winged dragon bookend on his desk. Was he struck with the matching one?" she asked.

"We believe so. The other bookend is missing, but the measurements of the remaining one matched up with the head wounds."

"Do you know if anything was stolen?" she asked.

"No money was found in the victim's wallet, but that doesn't mean he was robbed. I've known of wealthy people who never carry so much as a nickel on them."

The wallet would have been collected for evidence, she thought. "I can find out from Ike if there were any prints on the wallet other than the victim's," she said.

"Since when have you been calling George Eichle by his nickname?" Dan asked. "Are you two getting along better these days?"

"Much better. We're friends now."

"Your father will be pleased about that." Liz had to agree. She knew Pop and Ike had taken a liking to each other when Ike first made detective. The two of them had been partners before Pop retired. While she and Ike were in their hostile mode, his fondness for her father was like a spark of warmth in an ice storm.

Late as it was when she crawled into her sofa bed and turned out the light, she didn't fall asleep right away. A new homicide always activated her mind. She had to sort everything out.

The time frame of the murder was tight. Bruna had seen Maybanks go into his study at seven o'clock, right after his row with Emily. Her husband, Oleg, had discovered the body at half-past-ten.

Why did Oleg go to the study at half-past-ten? Ike would have asked him about that during the interview. Oleg probably had a good reason for going to the study so late in the evening. Most likely he brought Maybanks something from the kitchen every night at that hour—a drink, maybe. Besides, if he'd committed the murder, where would he have stashed the bookend? Before she and Dan left the scene, the police had searched the servants' quarters, along with all the other rooms except the family bedrooms, and didn't find it. Besides, what would his motive have been? Robbery? Her original idea of a robber entering the study from the balcony seemed more likely. Tomorrow, she'd run both ideas past Ike. Suddenly a restless feeling came over her, a feeling of urgency. She wished she didn't have to wait until tomorrow to discuss the case with him. Had the missing bookend been found, after she and Dan left? Meanwhile, she could only review her own observations.

During her years of following homicides, she'd learned never to rule out anyone. Pop used to tell her the killer sometimes turned out to be the least likely suspect—maybe not a suspect at all, in the initial stages of the case.

She thought of Bruna. Maybe she'd gone to the study during the evening to try and persuade Maybanks not to take Emily's cat away from her. She obviously didn't like him. The discussion might have turned ugly.

And Mrs. Maybanks. She'd seemed more distraught about her daughter's disappearance than her husband's death. Chances were she wasn't fond of a husband who summoned her as if she were a lackey, and, according to Bruna, wasn't nice to her. What if she secretly harbored intense hatred for him and it had been festering for years and tonight it had come to a head? As for Kevin—he'd seemed upset about his sister. He'd seemed unwilling to accept the possibility that she might have run away. Could his sympathy and concern for her have led him to go to the study after dinner and ask his father to let Emily keep her cat? Could they have quarreled? Could it have become physical, driving Kevin to pick up a bookend and strike his father in self-defense? Given the fondness between father and son, this seemed unlikely. Besides, what would he have done with the bookend? He hadn't left the building, and he'd been more than willing for the police to search his bedroom. If he'd thrown it down the trash chute, the cops would have found it.

Emily. Bruna had seen her run to her mother's room after the confrontation with her father. She might have stayed there awhile, being comforted, and then told her mother she was going to bed. Instead, she'd gone to her father's study to plead with him to let her keep Patches. If he'd told her, again, he intended to have her beloved pet destroyed, she might have lost control. The time element fit. She could have killed her father anywhere between the time she left her mother's bedroom and the time she left the building. That could be what happened to the missing bookend. She could have taken it out in the cat carrier and dumped it somewhere. The bookend's weight wouldn't have been too much for her. It was the bronze dragon's sharp wings and tail that made it a lethal weapon.

Was Emily strong enough to bring the bookend down on her father's head with enough force to kill him? Liz recalled the family pictures in the study. Emily looked anything but robust. But she'd followed enough homicides to know the effect of rage-induced adrenaline. Ike knew it, too. This might explain why Ike hadn't seemed impatient when Emily's disappearance slowed his investigation. He intended to question Mrs. Maybanks about what time Emily had left, supposedly to go to her own room. Emily might be a suspect.

Again, she felt the need to discuss her ideas with him.

When she finally fell asleep, it was with the hope that he wouldn't wait too long to get in touch with her.

THREE

NEWS OF GREGORY MAYBANKS'S murder was on TV the next morning. Liz watched and listened while making coffee and toasting a bagel. Other than reading an obituary, and mentioning that the murder weapon had not yet been found, the newscaster had little to report. Apparently the media had not been told about Emily's disappearance.

She folded up the sofa bed and sat down with her bagel and coffee to continue watching the coverage of the murder. A shot of the Maybankses' apartment building came on, showing a throng of news reporters and camera crews clustered outside the police barricade.

"Stand by for a live interview with Dr. Elliott Ray, the Maybankses' family physician," the female newscaster said. "Dr. Ray has been at the Maybankses' apartment since early this morning. He has agreed to answer a few questions."

A camera panned in on a middle-aged man emerging from the entrance. There was something familiar about his face, Liz thought.

"Dr. Ray—you've been the Maybankses' family physician for many years and you were a close friend of Gregory Maybanks—is that right?" the interviewer asked.

The doctor appeared shaken, but his voice sounded calm.

"Yes," he replied. "I've been taking care of the Maybanks family ever since I started to practice. My friendship with Mr. Maybanks goes back to our college days."

In a flash, Liz knew why he looked familiar. He was one of the young men in the photographs she'd seen last night in the study. Take away the youthful sideburns and chin-length hair and there was no doubt about it. He had the same round, affable face.

"How is the family taking this terrible tragedy?" the interviewer asked.

"They're bearing up very well. I was attending a meeting out of town last night and didn't get word till very late—or I should say very early this morning. I hurried over here right away and stayed with the family till now. I intended to prescribe a sedative for Mrs. Maybanks, but she doesn't need it. She's remarkably composed."

"How are the children doing?"

"The son's upset, of course. He and his father were very close."

"And the daughter?"

"Dazed, I don't think it's fully sunk in, yet." His words startled Liz. Emily was home! She must have returned during the night. If Ike had still been at the apartment when she came back, they'd have a lot to discuss.

Onscreen, the doctor was winding up the questioning.

"And now, if you'll excuse me, I must be on my way," he said.

An unusually agreeable man, to go on TV and answer questions after a close friend had just been murdered, Liz thought. He probably hadn't had any sleep, either.

Reporters shouted more questions, but the coverage ended. In the studio, a newscaster advised viewers to stay tuned for breaking developments.

The doctor must have known that Emily was gone from the apartment for several hours last night. And if Ike had still been there when the doctor arrived, they'd talked. Obviously the doctor was very close to the family. Liz guessed he knew everything there was to know about them, including Gregory Maybanks's ill treatment of everyone in the household except Kevin. Dr. Ray probably knew the reason for this. She'd picked up enough about Maybanks to sense that his partiality toward his son might be part of a family secret, and Dr. Ray knew the whole of it.

Suddenly she felt consumed with the need to know it, too. If only there were some way she could talk to this doctor.

When an idea popped into her mind, she decided to go with it. She picked up the phone and called Dan.

"Well, good morning, Lizzie," Dan said. "I know you've been watching the news and you saw the Maybankses' family doctor. I guess you were surprised to hear the daughter came home last night, after we left."

"Yes, and I was wondering—do you know Dr. Elliott Ray?"

"I don't know him well, but we've met several times at County Medical Society functions."

"He's not a specialist, is he? He's in Family Practice?" A note of suspicion sounded in Dan's voice. "Yes. Why?"

"I want to go and see him as a patient. I'd like to tell him you recommended him to me."

"What are you up to, Lizzie?"

"I want to talk to him."

"You mean you want to question him about the Maybanks family. Forget it, Lizzie. Remember doctor-patient confidentiality. He wouldn't tell you anything."

"If I could get him talking he might let something slip. That's why I want to mention your name. Working for the Medical Examiner would be an opening wedge in the conversation."

Dan was silent for a moment. "Well, I guess there'd be no harm in it," he said.

"Oh, thanks, Dan. I'm going to make an appointment with Dr. Ray for a physical checkup. Do you think his office would be open today?"

"Ordinarily, a Family Practice office would be open Saturdays, but don't forget, he just lost a close friend, and he's been up all night. And even if he hasn't cancelled office hours today, you probably wouldn't be able to get in on such short notice. You could make your appointment, but it might not be for a couple of weeks. Good luck. Let me know how it turns out."

She hung up the phone feeling discouraged. She'd hoped to see Dr. Ray in a couple of days, not a couple of weeks, but she'd give it a try, anyway.

The office was open. The nurse said the doctor would be in, later. But Dan was right—he was booked until a week from next Friday. She didn't make the appointment, but asked the nurse to phone her if there was a cancellation for sometime within the next few days.

She felt plagued with frustration. She'd been keyed up at the prospect of talking to Dr. Ray. She'd planned to mention that she'd been at the Maybankses' house the night of the murder. That might start him talking about his friendship with Gregory Maybanks. She wanted to find out if Maybanks always had a mean streak, or if something had happened to make him that way. But, even more, she wanted to uncover the secret she sensed within this dysfunctional family.

She decided to work off her frustration by cleaning the apartment. Dressed in old jeans and shirt, she dusted the furniture and ran the vacuum cleaner over the carpet, wishing she could have made an appointment with Dr. Ray for Monday or Tuesday. She scoured the kitchen sink and swept the small patch of vinyl flooring that separated it from the carpeted area. She'd just finished a mop job on the bathroom floor when the phone rang.

Could that be Ike? She hastened to pick up.

It was Dr. Ray's office nurse. His first scheduled patient had just cancelled. Could she possibly get there in an hour? Dr. Elliott Ray had to be truly dedicated to his patients to hold office hours so soon after his close friend had been murdered, Liz thought, as she took a quick shower. He sounded like old Doc Blumberg who'd taken care of her and her family on Staten Island. According to Gram, who still lived there, he'd made house calls until the day he retired.

She put on dark blue slacks and white shirt. The weather forecast promised cool temperatures all day, so she looked around for her blue wool blazer. In her tiny apartment, if something didn't show up quickly, that meant it wasn't there. Then she remembered she'd worn the blazer last night and taken it off in Gregory Maybanks's study. It must still be there, hanging on the arm of the chair. Unless it had been bagged as evidence. But that wasn't likely, she decided. The cops had finished gathering evidence in the study before she and Dan got there.

She put on a sweater instead. Retrieving her blazer would give her an excuse to go back to the Maybankses' apartment, she thought, as she locked her apartment door and started down the stairs. But first things first. After a talk with Dr. Ray, she'd think about getting her blazer.

In the lower hall, Rosa Moscaretti opened the door of her apartment.

"Hello, Dearie," she called. "Where are you off to?"

Rosa and her husband, Joe, were such great people, she couldn't think of them as nosy. They were just interested in her and her well-being. "I have a doctor's appointment," she replied. "Sorry I can't stop and chat, but I'm in a big hurry."

FACE TO FACE WITH Dr. Ray, she noticed he looked weary.

He couldn't have had more than a couple of hours' sleep before coming to the office, she thought. He was a throwback to the era before medical specialization, when the same physician treated a patient head to toe, and the family doctor was a family friend.

After a routine physical exam, the nurse ushered her into the doctor's consulting room. He looked up from the form she'd filled out in the reception room.

"You're in good shape, Elizabeth," he said. "You look younger than twenty-three. You could pass for a teenager. You're underweight, though. Are you eating enough?"

Liz thought of the sketchy meals she'd been eating since Mom and Pop moved to Florida. Morning coffee on the run. Takeout or fast food for lunch. Microwaved frozen dinners. If it weren't for eating out now and then with Sophie, or an occasional dinner date, she might be even thinner.

"I don't eat as well as I did before I moved into my own place," she said. "My parents live in Florida now."

He nodded. "You're nowhere near being danger-ously underweight, but I'd like to have you put on a few pounds. Let's say five, but I'd rather see ten. How's your appetite?"

She laughed, remembering her last dinner date. Phil Perillo had taken her to the Rainbow Room, where she'd polished off a jumbo shrimp cocktail, Beef Wellington with all the trimmings, a big salad and a fancy dessert. "After a good restaurant meal there's never a scrap left on my plate for a doggy bag," she replied.

"Cooking for one and eating alone is the problem," he said. "Try having a friend over for a meal once a week or so. It wouldn't have to be fancy—just good, nourishing food like your mother used to feed you. That might help to get your eating habits back in line. And if you're not taking vitamins, I want you to start. One multi a day will be fine."

He glanced at the information form again. "I see Dr. Switzer recommended me. And you work for him. It must be an interesting job, working for the M. E."

She decided to get right to what she'd come here for, before her allotted time ran out. "Yes, it's very interesting. Dr. Switzer often takes me along to crime scenes. Last night I went to the Maybankses' apartment. I guess you heard about the murder."

A grim expression crossed the doctor's face. His shoulders sagged. "Gregory Maybanks was a longtime friend of mine," he said. "I've been the family doctor for many years."

She'd planned to question him about Maybanks—after expressing her condolences, of course. She had every intention of finding out what kind of a college boy

Maybanks had been, if he'd always had a mean streak, or if something had happened to turn him into a man who wasn't civil to anyone in his household except his son. But suddenly she knew she couldn't go on with this deception. Dr. Ray seemed to be a thoroughly good man. He didn't deserve to be used.

"I'm sorry you lost your friend," she said. "Especially in such a terrible way."

"I appreciate your sympathy," he replied.

If she hadn't decided to let it go, this would have been the right moment for her to squeeze in the first of a few discreet questions. She let the moment pass.

"According to the detectives at the Maybankses' apartment, the cause of death is believed to be two blows to the head with a bronze bookend," the doctor said. "The bookend used as the weapon is missing."

"Right. Dr. Switzer told me the other one matched up with the wounds."

A grave expression crossed the doctor's face. He nodded, then gave a wan smile. "Well, as I said, you're in excellent health, Elizabeth. My nurse will phone you if anything shows up on your test results. Unless there's some problem, I don't need to see you again for a year."

"That will give me time to gain some weight," she said, rising from her chair.

He got to his feet, saying, "Good thinking."

What a nice man, she thought, as she left the office. She might have missed her chance to delve deeper into Gregory Maybanks's personality and the secret she was sure he harbored, but whatever regret she felt about that was preferable to the guilt she'd feel if she used him.

While she walked to the subway, her thoughts returned to her blazer. Should she go to the Maybankses' apartment and get it, now? No, she decided. Without Dan, she wouldn't get past the police barricades. Maybe if she phoned and spoke to Bruna, Bruna would remember her from last night and get word to the security guard that it was okay to let her into the building. But she couldn't be sure Bruna wouldn't take the blazer to the lobby and leave it with the doorman.

She couldn't risk this opportunity to get inside the Maybankses' apartment again. Somehow, she'd think of a way.

She was still thinking about it when she got to her apartment building. She still hadn't come up with a workable plan.

The moment she entered the building, the door to the Moscarettis' apartment opened. "How did it go at the doctor, Dearie?" Rosa asked.

"Fine, Rosa. It was just a routine checkup."

"I was sure that's what it was. That's what I told your cop friend. 'Don't worry,' I said. 'My husband and I would know if Liz was sick.'"

Liz stared at her. "Detective Eichle was here?"

"About half an hour ago. I was reading the morning paper, when I heard someone come in the front door."

The Moscarettis' building didn't have a buzzer entry system, but with Rosa and Joe on the premises, it didn't need one.

"I told him he was welcome to wait for you here," Rosa said. "I offered him coffee, but he said he just came by to tell you something and he couldn't stay. Such a nice young man, Dearie. I could tell he was worried about you. He said he'd phone you."

"Thanks, Rosa." Liz climbed the stairs, wondering if Ike had really been worried about her. Probably not. It had been too short a time since they'd progressed from hostility to civility, and then to friendship. Their friendship was too new. It hadn't reached the stage where he'd be concerned about her seeing a doctor.

She'd only been inside her place for a few minutes when the phone rang. No name came up on the caller ID. She didn't want to get involved with a Saturday telemarketer. She let it ring and went into her kitchenette. It was almost lunchtime. She felt hungry. There wasn't much in the fridge for her to begin taking Dr. Ray's advice, but maybe a peanut butter sandwich would do for starters.

The answering machine clicked on. She heard Ike's voice. "Liz—are you okay? I dropped by your place a little while ago and your landlady told me you'd gone to a doctor."

She should have remembered Ike's cell phone didn't identify him by name. She rushed to pick up.

"I'm here, Ike, and I'm okay. I went to the doctor for a routine physical, that's all." She decided not to tell him, yet, that the doctor was Dr. Elliott Ray. There'd be time for that, later.

"Good," he said. "Your landlady had me worried for

a couple of minutes before she told me she was sure it wasn't anything serious."

That sounded as if he'd really been concerned about her, she thought, feeling pleased. "I'm sorry I missed you, Ike. Anything new?"

"Yeah. The daughter came back after you left."

"I saw the Maybankses' doctor on TV this morning. From what he said, I gathered Emily was home when he got there. It must have been rough, breaking the news about her father. How did she take it?"

"She seemed dazed—as if she didn't quite get it." Liz recalled that Dr. Ray had made much the same observation.

"Where did she go last night?"

"The Maybanks have a maid who comes in by the day. Evidently Emily's fond of her. She went to the maid's place."

"And the maid sent her home?"

"She brought Emily home in a taxi to make sure she got there okay."

"She sounds like a good person."

"Right, she's a young Haitian woman. Name's Mariette. I talked to her for a while. I got an earful."

"Are you going to share the earful with me?"

"That's what I intended to do when I dropped by."

He didn't want to discuss it on the phone. "When can you come over again?" she asked.

"Not till tomorrow. I'll call you." She hung up the phone, feeling excitement and anticipation. Prospects of getting in on important homicide case information always affected her this way. She might have felt frustrated, having to wait until tomorrow to find out what Ike had picked up from the Haitian maid, but she wasn't. He'd given her something extra to think about.

He really had been worried about her!

FOUR

THE REST OF THE DAY and the entire evening stretched out before Liz like a blank sheet of paper. It was one of those Saturdays when Sophie was working all day and they couldn't get together. No date for tonight, either, but that was nothing unusual. Regular Saturday night dates were for the firmly committed, and there was no man in her life at present who answered that description.

But, being between boyfriends wasn't so bad. It was certainly preferable to being hassled by someone who didn't approve of her interest in following homicides. She was surprised how relieved she felt after she broke up with Wade, a month or so ago. Sure, she missed the dinner dates and seeing all the latest Broadway shows, but she didn't miss Wade's arrogance and dictatorial attitude at all.

She sat down with her notebook to review the notes she'd made in the Maybankses' apartment and to add what she'd found out during her visit to Dr. Ray. If he hadn't come across as such a nice man, she wouldn't have held back with her questions. She might have picked up something. Now, she didn't know anymore than she'd learned from the doctor's TV interview.

He'd given her some good medical advice, though.

She had to agree she should gain some weight. A few more five-star restaurant dates with Phil Perillo would help. Suddenly she remembered she had a date with Phil for next Friday night. Strange that it had slipped her mind. Guys like Phil didn't come along often. The combination of good looks, terrific sense of humor and a fondness for fine dining should have made him unforgettable.

Dr. Ray had suggested having a friend over for dinner now and then. That might improve her eating habits, he'd said. Well, it would be a way of getting something into her fridge besides frozen dinners. Since she'd been on her own in New York, even burgers and franks had become gourmet fare.

A thought sprang into her mind. When Ike phoned her tomorrow, she'd ask him to come for dinner. That meant she'd have to buy some real groceries today. An unmarried detective would recognize a frozen dinner at twenty paces, even if she scooped it out of the container and served it in one of the fancy dishes Gram had given her. Besides, she'd established a standard. Recently, in an attempt to pry some information out of him about his last murder case, she'd fed him a sirloin steak dinner with all the trimmings.

Tomorrow she'd have spaghetti, she decided. For dessert, she had lemon sherbet in the freezer. She decided to go to the market today. She started making out a shopping list.

Ready to go, she picked up her purse and put on a sweater. Her blazer was still in Gregory Maybanks's study. Well, it could stay there till she decided how she could use it to get back inside the apartment.

WHEN SHE RETURNED from the market, Rosa greeted her in the downstairs hall. There was no way Rosa could miss the long loaf of Italian bread sticking out of the grocery sack, or the other bag emblazoned with the name of the wine shop.

"Looks like you're having company, Dearie," she said.

"Yes—tomorrow night," Liz replied. She started up the stairs before Rosa could peer into the grocery sack and see the jar of pasta sauce and the cardboard container of grated cheese.

Liz knew Rosa's opinion of store-bought pasta sauce.

The only kind worthy of eating had to be concocted from scratch and simmered until the area around her stove looked like the scene of an axe murder. As for the cheese—you might as well be sprinkling sawdust on your pasta unless you'd nicked your knuckles grating a wedge of Romano.

Sophie would probably have to learn how to cook Italian after she married Ralph, she thought, as she let herself into her apartment. Ralph came from a big, Italian-American family. His mother was probably just like Rosa. But somehow, she couldn't picture feisty Sophie Pulaski taking any flak from a mother-in-law.

The thought of Ralph made her think of Phil Perillo. Phil and Ralph were cousins. But Phil had told her his mother was Irish. That accounted for his Gaelic charm and blarney, she decided. An Irish mother might not have any problem with store-bought pasta sauce. Maybe Phil had been weaned on food products straight from the market shelves or freezer, but he'd developed into a real gourmet.

Had Ike grown up with a mother who cooked from scratch? Eichle sounded like a German name. Sauerbraten and Weiner schnitzel. As far as she knew, there was nothing like that, ready to go.

What had led her into this train of thought? she asked herself, as she unpacked the groceries. She hadn't the remotest intention of taking on any kind of mother-in-law.

Ike phoned her at half-past-two the next day.

"OKAY IF I COME OVER later on?" he asked.

"Sure. Come for dinner."

"Thanks, Liz—that'll be great." She could tell by his ready reply and the tone of his voice that he remembered the last dinner she'd cooked for him. "No sirloin steak this time," she warned. "I hope you like spaghetti."

"One of my favorites. If you're as good with spaghetti as you are with steak, I know I'm in for a treat."

She hung up the phone feeling vaguely disturbed. "If you're as good with spaghetti…" He wasn't picturing sauce out of a jar and cheese out of a cardboard carton.

Suddenly she wished Rosa had seen what was in her grocery bag and insisted on giving her a bowl of her freshly made sauce. It wasn't too late. She knew if she went down to the Moscarettis' apartment now and confided in Rosa…

She shook her head. Why was getting herself in a tizzy? This wasn't gourmet Phil Perillo coming to dinner. It was only Ike. Besides, Mom had shown her how to jazz up store-bought sauce so it tasted almost as good as something out of a Neapolitan kitchen.

She opened up the gate leg table she only used when she had guests. In this one room apartment, her kitchen area consisted of sink, stove and fridge lined up behind a screen. No room for a table. When she was alone, she carried a tray to her sofa bed and ate there.

Mom used to put a red-and-white checked cloth on the table whenever she made a spaghetti dinner. Liz wished she had it, or one like it, tonight. She settled for one of the tablecloths Mom gave her before taking off for Florida. Plain white. But it was more in keeping with a spaghetti dinner than the lace cloth Gram gave her as an apartment-warming gift.

Why was she making such a big deal about Ike coming for dinner? It was sort of an occasion, she told herself. In addition to the dinner she'd cooked for him while trying to pry information out of him, they'd gone out for pizza once, they'd had a deli lunch and even one restaurant dinner. But this was the first time they would eat together as declared friends. Besides feeling indebted to her for her help in his past couple of cases, being friends was a plus. She was sure he'd tell her more about the Maybanks case than he would have before.

"THE SPAGHETTI smells good," Ike said, settling himself on the sofa.

"It's ready any time you are," she replied.

"I should have brought some wine. Sorry. I'll do better next time."

"I have that covered," she replied. "I need you to open it for me, though. I always seem to get pieces of cork in the bottle."

He followed her behind the screen into the kitchen area. While she dished up the spaghetti and sauce, he opened the wine and poured it into goblets.

At the table, he raised his glass. "Here's to solving the Maybanks case."

"And here's to you letting me in on what you found out since yesterday," she said.

"I was getting to that." He paused to shake some grated cheese over his spaghetti. "We still haven't found the murder weapon, which we believe is the missing bookend. It didn't turn up anywhere in the apartment."

Again Liz pictured Emily taking the missing bookend out of the apartment in her cat carrier. But it was hard to establish Emily in her mind as a suspect without meeting her, face-to-face. She had to get back into the Maybankses' apartment, somehow. Before she could express her thoughts about Emily, Ike continued.

"I told you I had a talk with the Haitian maid, Mariette," he said. "She speaks English fairly well. I gathered she's no fan of Gregory Maybanks. She likes Mrs. Maybanks, though, and she's very fond of Emily."

"I'd say Emily was fond of her, too, running to her

the way she did. It's as if Mariette's the only person she could turn to."

Ike nodded. "Poor kid didn't dare bring the cat home with her. Left it at Mariette's place, like she was sure her father would have it taken to the pound and put down, first thing in the morning."

"Sounds like Mariette has a soft spot for Emily, but what did she have to say about Kevin? Does she like him?"

"She seemed to. When I mentioned him, she dropped a French phrase I didn't fully catch. I know she said *charmant,* and I'm pretty sure that means charming, but the other part sounded like *trumpet.* How's your French, Liz?"

She laughed. "Rusty. Sounds like Kevin charmed people with his trumpet playing."

"It's probably nothing, but I'll get hold of a French dictionary when I have the time and try and figure it out."

"What else did Mariette say?"

"Plenty. She told me she finished her work Friday evening around six and on her way to the elevator she heard voices in Maybanks's study. The door was closed, but it sounded like an argument, she said."

"Did she have any idea who might be in there?"

"She said she recognized Maybanks's voice. He was doing most of the talking. The other voice wasn't loud enough to recognize but she thought it was a man's."

Liz took a sip of wine. Thanks to the information from the security guard, Ike knew nobody had come into the apartment on Friday evening after Kevin arrived home from school shortly before six. The only men in the apartment the entire evening were Oleg and Kevin.

"Maybanks wouldn't have been arguing with Kevin. Bruna told me Kevin was the only one in the household he was nice to," she said.

Ike nodded. "Mariette said that, too. But get this. The argument took place just before dinner. Oleg served at the table. I asked him if Maybanks seemed angry toward any particular family member during the meal. He said—and I'll quote him, Slavic accent and all— 'The boss, he all the time angry with Madam and Emily, but tonight he angry with Kevin.'"

"Wow—that sounds as if Kevin was the one involved in the argument."

"He was. When I questioned him he admitted it. He said his father was angry because he let his grades slip after he was accepted at Princeton. I didn't buy it. Maybanks wouldn't have been that angry over a slip from A's to B's."

Why had Kevin lied? This made him seem guilty. But Liz hadn't ruled out Oleg. "I've never met Oleg," she said. "What's he like?"

"Withdrawn. But that could be due to the shock of finding the body."

"Do you consider him a strong suspect?"

"Not as it stands now. We couldn't come up with a motive. We thought Maybanks might have been holding some immigration violation over Oleg's head, but when we checked with INS, there was nothing irregular. Both he and Bruna admitted they didn't like Maybanks, personally, but they have no beef with their jobs. They said they're getting top wages with adequate time off, and their living quarters are comfortable."

"Everything points to Kevin, doesn't it?"

Ike twirled several strands of spaghetti around his fork. "As far as arguing with his father in the study is concerned—yes, but that doesn't prove he went back in there later and killed him. Actually, he's less of a suspect than Emily. She had an argument with her father earlier, too, and what's more, she had a motive. He was going to have her cat put down."

"If Emily did it, she could have taken the missing bookend out of the apartment in her cat carrier."

She could tell by his smile he'd thought of this himself. "Good thinking," he said. "Mariette's apartment was searched as soon as we found out that's where Emily went, but nothing turned up in her place or in the cat carrier, either."

Liz nodded. Emily would have gotten rid of the bookend on her way to Mariette's apartment.

"We have cops searching trash bins in the area where Mariette lives," Ike said.

"Is the cat back with Emily?" Liz asked.

"Yes. Mariette brought it back yesterday. The carrier's at the Police lab now. If the murder weapon was ever in it, traces of blood and hair will show up."

Liz nodded. "Emily probably had a cushion in the carrier for Patches. There'd be evidence all over it."

"There was a cushion. We're holding off further questioning of Emily till the lab report comes back."

"Have you questioned Kevin again, about the argument with his father?"

"Not yet. We plan to do follow-up questioning of everyone in the household. Probably tomorrow."

That meant the servants and family members were all under suspicion, Liz thought. She realized she'd been so caught up with Emily and Kevin, she hadn't given much thought to their mother.

"How did the interview go with Mrs. Maybanks?" she asked.

"She was very cooperative."

"Did she express any ideas? I mean, how the killer could have gotten into the apartment and what the motive was?"

"She thinks someone gained access by way of the fire stairs. She believes it was planned as a robbery but ended in homicide when her husband put up a fight."

"How could that happen? I thought doors opening onto fire stairs could only be used as exits."

"Right. It's strictly one-way. And you saw the body. You know Maybanks wasn't putting up any fight. He was sitting at his desk. When I pointed these facts out to her, she said she didn't know how else it could have happened."

Naturally, Mrs. Maybanks wouldn't suspect her children or her devoted servants, Liz thought. But didn't Ike think her answer was vague? Mrs. Maybanks could have committed this murder herself. She certainly didn't seem to be grieving. Ike must have considered this angle, even though they hadn't discussed it. They had so much to discuss.

She noticed Ike was down to his last few strands of spaghetti. "There's more where that came from," she said. "How about a refill?"

He flashed a big smile. "I was hoping you made enough for seconds." He followed her into the kitchen area.

At the stove, she refilled his dish. This would be a good time to tell him she wanted to see Emily Maybanks face-to-face, she decided.

"I want to go back to the Maybankses' apartment," she said, spooning sauce onto his pasta. "I want to get a handle on Emily. I've never seen her—only her photograph."

She knew she didn't have to elaborate. He'd understand she wanted to judge for herself if Emily had the strength to bash her father's head in with the bronze dragon.

He waited until they sat down at the table again before replying. "You know if I could take you to the apartment with me, I would."

She nodded, "I know." He'd already let her in on details that hadn't been released to the media yet. She didn't expect anymore than that.

She told him about leaving her blazer in Maybanks's study. "Could I use that as an excuse? I could phone Bruna and say I'm coming to pick it up."

His reply sounded discouraging. "You could try."

"You mean Bruna could take it down to the lobby and leave it with the doorman? I thought of that, but don't you think there's a chance Bruna or Mrs. Maybanks would have me come to the apartment? I had a very friendly talk with Bruna on Friday night, and Mrs. Maybanks was friendly, too."

"I wouldn't count on it, Liz."

She sighed. "Going there for my blazer is the only way I can think of to see Emily—maybe even talk to her."

"Even if it worked out that you got into the apartment to pick it up, that's no guarantee you'd see Emily," he said. "But cheer up, I have an idea. I can't take you to the apartment with me, but I can take you to the funeral. You can see Emily there."

"Are you serious?"

"Sure. We don't know yet when it'll be, but you can count on it."

"Oh, thanks a million, Ike! That will be perfect. It will give me a chance to observe her."

"I intend to do some observing myself," he said. "I know from experience, a lot can be learned at funerals."

After their lemon sherbet dessert, they went to the sofa to drink their coffee.

"That was a great feed, Liz," he said, leaning back onto Gram's floral needlepoint pillows and stretching his long legs out. "If I ate like this every night I'd be a walrus. How do you manage to stay slim?"

"I don't eat like this every night, either." She meant to leave it at that, but found herself saying, "I guess I should. Dr. Ray thinks I'm too thin. He wants me to put on a few pounds."

The instant she said it she remembered she hadn't told him that she'd deliberately planned a checkup with the Maybankses' family physician.

"Dr. Ray? Dr. Elliott Ray?" The look he gave her told her he knew exactly what she'd done. But he seemed more surprised than disturbed. That was a good sign.

"Yes," she replied. "I might as well tell you I knew when I made my appointment for a checkup that he was the Maybankses' family doctor. I saw him on TV."

"So you decided to have a checkup and pump him for information about the Maybanks family. Hitting two birds with one stone."

He didn't look angry or even annoyed, but he wasn't smiling, either.

"I was going to tell you about it tonight, but we started talking about so many other things, it slipped my mind," she said. "I didn't find out anything, anyway. If I did, I would have remembered, and told you." She paused, searching his face for signs of displeasure. "Are you mad at me for trying to do some investigating on my own?"

To her relief, he smiled. "I got over that two homicides ago," he replied. "At least this time you didn't get yourself into a dangerous situation."

"Far from it. Dr. Ray's a nice man—too nice to be hoodwinked by questions. I didn't ask him any. That's why I didn't get any information."

"Yeah, he's an okay guy. I guess you heard him say on TV that he's known Maybanks for many years."

"Yes. He also mentioned it while I was in his office. And while I was at the crime scene I noticed some photos on the wall. Maybanks and Dr. Ray and another fellow—when they were in college, I guess. The three of them looked as if they were close buddies."

"They were. Still are. The third guy is Conrad Schuler, now the Maybankses' attorney. He lives in the same building. He came right down to the Maybankses' apartment as soon as he got word of the homicide. We interviewed him the same time as Dr. Ray."

Liz recalled the photographs in the study. Three carefree college pals. Nothing about Maybanks to suggest he had a mean streak. If he did, would the other two have stayed friends with him all these years?

"Did you find out anything about Maybanks in his younger days?" she asked.

"According to Schuler and Ray, he was an okay kid. If you're wondering if something happened later, to make him such a stinker, serving two years in Vietnam could have done it. He was ROTC in college and went right into the army when he graduated. He saw a lot of action. Got the Bronze Star and the Purple Heart."

"The Purple Heart. Did they say how he was wounded?"

"He got zapped by a punji stick—one of those poisoned arrows the Vietcong buried along the trails. Lucky the one that got Maybanks had been in the ground awhile and the poison lost some of its potency, otherwise he might have died."

Whatever the poisoned arrow did to Maybanks, Liz

was sure this had soured him on life and almost everyone in it.

"Did they say he came back from Vietnam a changed man?" she asked.

"No. They said he seemed all right when he first got back. He started his real estate and construction business and it took off right away. He'd already made his first million when they noticed a change in his personality. He became antisocial, they said. Dropped all his friends except them. Did nothing but work. They were surprised and pleased when he got married a few years later. They hoped his wife would be able get him back on track."

"But that didn't happen."

"No. Instead, the situation got worse. He drew himself even further into his shell."

"Did they say anything about Mrs. Maybanks, or the marriage?"

"Mrs. Maybanks was a clerk in Schuler's law office. That's how she and Maybanks met. Schuler said she was a nice, quiet woman about the same age as Maybanks. Never married before."

"Poor woman—she didn't know what she was getting into—marrying someone so antisocial."

"It must have been rough on her. He never took her out anywhere and wouldn't allow her to invite anyone to their home. The only people he'd have anything to do with outside of business were Ray and Schuler. But that didn't include their wives, so Mrs. Maybanks had virtually no social life. She never went anywhere except church. She did have a few acquaintances from church, but under the circumstances she couldn't form any close friendships."

"I'm surprised he didn't object to her going to church."

"I guess he didn't care as long as it didn't involve him. He never attended services. He had one redeeming feature, though. He gave generous financial support to the church, and, according to his bank statements, he wasn't stingy with his wife and kids, either. Schuler and Ray backed this up. Mrs. Maybanks was always well-dressed, and she has a sable coat and a diamond solitaire the size of a cherry tomato."

Mrs. Maybanks would probably be willing to trade that cherry tomato for a normal life, Liz thought.

The phone rang. Most likely Mom and Pop. They always called her on Sunday nights. "This might be my folks," she said, picking up.

Pop's voice came over the line. "Hello, Lizzie."

"Hi, Pop. How're you doing, and how's Mom?"

Ike got to his feet. "I'll go. I know you want to talk to them."

"Don't go, yet. Pop will want to say hello to you."

She turned back to the phone. "Pop, your favorite detective's here," she said. "I'll put him on."

"George Eichle's there?" Pop sounded surprised. Also pleased.

Ike and Pop talked for a few minutes—the easy talk of two cops with respect and affection for one another.

Then Ike said, "Hold on, Frank, while I thank Liz for a great dinner. Then I'll put her on and hit the road."

"It *was* a great dinner," he told her, as he strode to the door. "I'll be in touch."

"Don't forget you promised to take me to the funeral," she said.

He nodded as he went out the door. "It's a date."

Only someone as hooked on homicides as she was could look forward to such a fun date.

IN BED, SHE REVIEWED what Ike had told her that evening. She was almost asleep, when she remembered something he'd said.

He'd mentioned that one of the three college pals, attorney Conrad Schuler, lived in the same building as the Maybankses', and that he came *down* as soon as he got word of the homicide. Of course that meant he lived in an apartment on one of the floors above.

Again, she thought of someone entering the study from the balcony. She fell asleep knowing she had to find out in what part of the building Schuler's apartment was, and if it, too, had a balcony.

FIVE

LIZ WAKENED THE NEXT morning to the sight and sound of rain pelting on her windows. Thoughts of Conrad Schuler were still in the forefront of her mind. While she showered and dressed, she reviewed the possibility that Schuler was the killer.

Suppose he lived in the apartment directly above. If his place had a balcony, he could have gotten down onto the balcony off Maybanks's study. If Maybanks had opened the doors to the balcony on that mild night, Schuler could have entered the study undetected. He could have bludgeoned Maybanks with the bookend and made his getaway, taking the murder weapon with him.

Even while this scenario spun in her head, she realized it didn't make much sense. Conrad Schuler was no gymnastic kid. Even if his balcony was directly above Maybanks's, he'd have to be Spider Man to pull it off. Besides, why would he want to kill his old friend?

THE EARLY TV NEWS REPORT on the murder of real estate tycoon Gregory Maybanks remained sketchy and repetitive. Death was believed to have been caused by one or more blows to the victim's head. The murder weapon was believed to be a bronze bookend. The bookend had not been found. Police had not yet come up with any suspects.

Taking the first gulp of her morning coffee, Liz listened and smiled. She loved being ahead of the headlines and the bulletins.

But how long would it take for some savvy investigative reporter to find a way of questioning the servants and getting to one of the security guards? If this happened, the media would find out about Emily leaving the apartment on the night of the murder. The tabloids would have a great time with that.

For lack of anything more sensational to report, the newscaster launched into an account of Gregory Maybanks's life and career.

"...Maybanks's meteoric rise in Manhattan real estate development began after he returned from army service in Vietnam..."

"...he married in 1985. He and his wife have a son and a daughter..."

Liz did some quick calculating. Maybanks must have been over forty years old when he got married. Mrs. Maybanks wasn't any spring chicken, either, when they tied the knot. They'd had their children much later in life than the average couple.

The weather report came on, predicting unseasonably low temperatures and heavy rain. Definitely a day for the raincoat and matching hat Mom and Pop gave her last Christmas.

She finished her coffee, grabbed her purse and raingear and headed for the door. Sorry, Dr. Ray—no time for a good breakfast this morning. She'd try and do better tomorrow.

A FEW MINUTES AFTER she got to her office, Dan came to her desk.

"I thought you might like to know we're winding up the autopsy on Maybanks today," he said.

How lucky she was to have a boss like Dan, she thought. When he retired his replacement would probably be someone who'd never discuss cases with her and thought her place was at the computer and nowhere else—especially not at crime scenes.

"Thanks," she said. "Has the missing dragon bookend definitely been established as the murder weapon?"

"It has," he replied. "There were two blows to the head. One showed a series of parallel stab wounds, evidently from sharp points on the dragon's wings. The other showed a deep wound matching the long, sharp end of the dragon's tail. Both blows were dealt with great force and caused severe skull damage, especially the stab from the tail."

Liz remembered the dragon's tail—long and coiled except for a straight, sharp area at the very end. Could Emily have brought it down with enough force to penetrate the skull? Seeing Emily in person would help her make that judgment.

"Will the body be released to the family today?" she asked.

"Most likely this afternoon."

"I guess the funeral will be Wednesday or Thursday.

May I have some time off to go to it? Ike said he'd take me."

"Sure, Lizzie." Dan looked at her with a curious smile. She knew he was thinking she and her former adversary were getting pretty cozy.

"By the way—how'd it go with Dr. Ray?" Dan asked.

"Okay. But he's such a nice man I couldn't bring myself to pump him for information when he was so broken up about his friend's death."

Dan smiled again as he turned to leave. "With you on such good terms with Detective Eichle lately, seems to me you didn't need to get information from Dr. Ray, after all," he said.

SOPHIE PHONED DURING the morning. Liz hoped she'd called to say Ralph was working that night. About the only time she and her best friend got together these days was when Sophie and Ralph couldn't.

"What's up?" she asked.

"I know Dan must have taken you to the Maybanks murder scene and I'm dying to hear all about it," Sophie replied. "I was hoping you were free for dinner tonight. Ralph's working."

"I'd like to tell you I have a date, but I'm free, as usual," Liz said with a laugh.

"What do you mean, 'as usual.' Aren't you going out with Phil Perillo this Friday night?"

Liz realized her upcoming date with Philadelphia Phil had again slipped her mind. The Maybanks case had crowded it out, she decided. "If Phil didn't come to New York once in a while, my dating average would be zero," she said.

Sophie laughed. "One date with Phil Perillo is worth ten of the regular kind."

Liz thought of last night's dinner with Ike. Was it actually a date? she asked herself. Did he think of it as a date? Suddenly she realized Sophie had been talking while she was lost in thought.

"Are you there, Liz?"

"I'm here. What were you saying?"

"We must have been cut off for a few seconds. I asked you where you want to eat tonight."

"You name it. You get around more than I do."

"There you go again. You're the one who's having another five-star date on Friday night."

Sophie was really pulling for something serious to develop with Phil, Liz thought.

They decided on a place in the East Village where they'd eaten a few times. Good home cooking served cafeteria-style, at a cost that wouldn't fracture their finances.

"I'll meet you there at six," Sophie said.

"THIS MUST BE the only place in town where the food tastes like something our mothers and grandmothers cooked," Liz said, after they settled themselves at a table with bowls of beef stew and plates of hot biscuits.

Sophie nodded. "Did you see all those wonderful desserts? If I'm still hungry after I finish this, I'm going back for that Boston cream pie."

"The strawberry cobbler looked awfully good, too." Liz said. "I like eating where we can afford dessert."

"Right. It's hard to find a reasonably priced place that isn't Mexican or Chinese, or something."

"It's fun to sample foreign foods once in a while, but give me good old American cooking any day," Liz replied.

"Does that include the Rainbow Room?" Sophie asked.

Another reference to Phil Perillo. "If you don't quit teasing me about Phil, I won't tell you about the Maybanks murder scene," Liz warned.

"Okay, I promise, not another word about him," Sophie said, buttering a biscuit. "So tell me what you know about the murder. I know Eichle's on the case with Lou Sanchez, but other than that I don't know much more than what's been on the news. I love being out where the action is, but I miss the squad room when there's been a big, baffling homicide."

How things had changed, Liz thought. Until a few weeks ago, Sophie was doing clerical work in Homicide. She kept her ears open, and when there was a case Liz wanted to follow, she passed information onto her. Now that she was a patrol cop, the situation was reversed. Besides this, there was another change. Sophie knew Ike had mellowed, but she didn't know, yet, that Eichle and Rooney were history, and they were calling each other Ike and Liz.

"It's a baffling case, all right," she said. "Maybe

things will start to unravel when the bookend turns up—if it ever does."

She could almost hear the wheels spinning in Sophie's head. Sophie had her sights set on becoming a Homicide detective. She'd be good at it. She knew how to put things together. "The killer couldn't leave the apartment to get rid of the bookend because the security guard would know who left the building and at what time," she said. "That makes it look like an inside job."

"Yes, one of the servants could have done it, or a family member," Liz said. "It didn't take me long to realize that Gregory Maybanks had a mean streak wide enough for almost everyone in the household to want him dead."

"Almost everyone? Who's the exception?"

"Kevin, the son. From what I picked up, he and his father got along very well."

"That leaves the servants, the daughter and Mrs. Maybanks," Sophie said. "The missing bookend has to be somewhere in the apartment. Where would the killer stash a large object like that to make sure it wouldn't be found right away?"

"It wasn't large. I saw the matching one on Maybanks's desk." She described it. "Dan said the tail did the most damage. It was like a dagger."

"Now that you and Eichle are getting along better, have you talked with him about the case? Does he suspect anyone in particular?"

"We tossed some ideas around last night, but so far nobody's been singled out."

After she said this she realized Sophie knew Ike wouldn't divulge any information over the phone. She was right.

"Last night?" Sophie asked. "Did he come over to your place?"

"He came for dinner. I was getting around to telling you we're friends now. We even call each other by our first names."

Sophie stared at her in disbelief. "I knew he'd loosened up, but this is a bombshell. Does this mean he'll let you in on everything that develops?"

"Maybe not everything, but a whole lot more than he did before. And he's taking me to the funeral." She told Sophie about wanting to see Emily in person.

"Sounds like the daughter's your own prime suspect," Sophie said.

"I haven't made up my mind about Emily yet, but…" She told Sophie her idea about Emily and the cat carrier.

"That would work," Sophie said. "But she's only thirteen. Is she a big, strong kid?"

"Not according to her photo. When I see her at the funeral, I'll know." She thought of her Spider Man idea, and laughed. "Here's a wild thought I had."

Sophie listened. "That might not be as wild as it sounds," she said. "It would explain why the murder weapon hasn't been found. Maybe this friend is very acrobatic. If his apartment has a balcony and if it's close enough, he could have rigged up a way to do it. Did you run the idea by Eichle?"

"No, I didn't tell Ike," Liz replied, emphasizing *Ike*.

"Ike," Sophie said. "That's going to take some getting used to. Why didn't you tell him about your Spider Man idea?"

"It seemed crazy, and anyway, this guy's an old college buddy of Maybanks's. They were very close. What would be his motive?"

"I can't imagine, but if I were you I'd let Ike in on this angle. He might dig something up."

"I'll probably see this friend at the funeral. I'll check him out for muscles before I say anything to Ike."

"Before you run it by Ike, you'd better check out the balconies, too, just to make sure this guy wouldn't really have to be Spider Man."

"I don't know what floor he lives on or if he even has a balcony. All I know is it's somewhere above the Maybankses' place."

"If you find out where the balconies are situated, then you can ask Ike what floor the guy lives on, and take it from there."

Liz glanced at her watch. "Good idea. I think I'll take a detour up to Park Avenue before I head home."

"Does that mean you're going to shell out for a cab instead of having dessert?" Sophie asked.

"No. I'm having dessert. The apartment's not too long a walk from the subway, and I'm dressed for walking in the rain."

"By the time you get there, it will still be light

enough for you to count the floors and see where the balconies are," Sophie said.

LIZ STOOD ACROSS the avenue from the Maybankses' apartment building. She could scrutinize it easily from here. The Maybankses' apartment was on the eighth floor. It would be easy to locate.

When she did, she was disappointed. The eighth floor had only one balcony. She recognized the French doors leading out from Maybanks's study. The floor above it had two, each located at opposite ends of the building, nowhere near the Maybankses' balcony.

Well, so much for that idea, she thought. But while she was here, she might as well go to the Maybankses' apartment and get her blazer. It didn't matter anymore if Bruna brought it down to the lobby. She'd be seeing Emily at the funeral.

She went to the traffic light at the end of the block, waited for the WALK signal and crossed the avenue. The rain had let up, but the sidewalk was crowded with scurrying pedestrians and umbrellas.

As she approached the apartment building, she noticed a burly young man with a head as bare and shiny as a billiard ball, standing near the entrance. She had a brief impression of a black, zip-up jacket, a sallow face and a cigarette dangling from a slack jaw. An instant later she saw Kevin Maybanks come out of the building. She was surprised when the two started talking.

She changed her mind about going in for her blazer. Some instinct told her not to let Kevin see her. She pulled the brim of her rain hat down and continued walking along among the umbrellas, past the entrance, past Kevin and the hairless stranger.

Though she got only a fleeting look at the bald-headed man, it was enough to tell her he couldn't possibly be a friend of Kevin's. He had the unmistakable look of a street punk. Pop would call him a hooligan.

SIX

WHY WOULD KEVIN MAYBANKS be talking with someone who looked like a wiseguy punk? The question
plagued her mind all the way to her subway stop and
continued after she got to her apartment.

Suddenly she recalled Ike telling her about a French
phrase Mariette had used to describe Kevin. One word
was *charmant.* That meant charming. The other word
sounded like *trumpet,* he'd said. If only she had a French
dictionary. Maybe if she concentrated, some of her high
school French would come back to her.

Trumpet... Trumpette... Trumpe... Trumpois... She
wasn't getting anywhere with this, but she'd keep trying.
Trumpelle... Trumpeur... Hold it! That last one almost
rang a bell. A moment later she had it. The word was
trompeur and it meant deceiver.

Mariette thought Kevin was a charming deceiver.
That could mean she liked him but didn't trust him.

Should she contact Ike tomorrow? she asked herself
as she opened her sofa bed for the night. Should she tell
him about Kevin and the hairless wise guy and about
Mariette's opinion of Kevin?

No, she decided. Pegging the hairless man as a
gangster might have been a mistake. It was her own
impression, just as Mariette's impression of Kevin as

a charming deceiver was hers. She'd already barked up one wrong tree. Or, in this case, one wrong balcony, she thought, with wry smile. Luckily, she hadn't told Ike about her Spider Man idea. Now that she had his respect for her investigative skills, she didn't want him changing his mind.

IKE CALLED HER AT WORK the next day. "The funeral service is tomorrow at three o'clock at St. Bartholomew's," he said. "I want to get there early. Can I pick you up outside your building at two?"

"The church is pretty far across town from my building," she replied. "Thanks for offering to pick me up, but I don't want to inconvenience you. I can get there on my own."

"At a high profile funeral like this one, there'll be cops stationed to keep the curiosity seekers away. You might have a hassle. Better let me come for you."

"Are you sure you don't mind going out of your way?"

"I'm sure."

"Okay. See you at two tomorrow."

She hung up the phone. *St. Bartholomew's. One of Manhattan's classiest churches.* And, mean-spirited as he was, Gregory Maybanks supported it generously. He was into magnanimous giving, she decided, recalling what Ike had told her about Mrs. Maybanks's sable coat and huge diamond ring.

What should she wear to the funeral service? She decided her navy blue skirt with a light blue blouse would do. Her blue blazer was still at the Maybankses' apartment. Her white cardigan sweater with yellow and blue flowers embroidered on wouldn't be too gaudy, but she remembered Gram saying that wearing anything except dark colors to a funeral was a sign of disrespect for the dead.

Why was she worrying about what to wear to the funeral of a man she wouldn't have respected if he were alive? She'd wear her flowered sweater.

THE AREA OUTSIDE the church was empty when she and Ike got there, but two uniformed cops were already posted at the entrance.

Would curious strangers actually try to attend the service? Liz wondered, as they approached the church. Gregory Maybanks wasn't a big Hollywood star or an important political figure. But with posh business and residential towers all over Manhattan bearing his name, he was a celebrity of sorts. Some people would want to see what his wife and children looked like. They'd want to gawk at important people who might be there.

Just as she was wondering how the cops would know the difference between friends and acquaintances of the Maybanks family and curious strangers, she saw Dr. Elliott Ray and another man come out of the church and speak to one of the cops.

The man with Dr. Ray must be Conrad Schuler, she thought. In her appraisal of him it was clear this sparely built, slightly stoop-shouldered man couldn't have pulled a Spider Man maneuver if the balconies were six inches apart.

He and Dr. Ray were going to screen everyone, she

decided. That wouldn't be difficult. From what she'd learned about Gregory Maybanks, his only friends were the two old college buddies. Most likely the funeral would be attended by business associates, dignitaries and people who knew Mrs. Maybanks and the children.

The two men recognized Ike right away from their interviews in the Maybankses' apartment.

"You're here early, Detective," Schuler said.

"I wanted to be the first one on the scene," Ike replied.

Liz halfway expected him to add, "The early bird catches the worm." She remembered what he'd said about picking up a lot at funerals.

She wasn't surprised when Dr. Ray didn't remember her at first. It wasn't until after he'd gestured for them to enter the church that a look of recognition crossed his face. "You were in my office a few days ago, weren't you?" he asked.

She nodded. If he remembered she worked for the Medical Examiner and wondered what she was doing here with a Homicide detective, he made no comment.

Inside the church, a closed casket, draped with an American flag, stood below the altar, flanked by urns of white roses. No viewing of the deceased. There'd be no burial service at a cemetery, either. She'd read in the newspaper that the body would be taken for cremation directly from the church. It was as if Mrs. Maybanks wanted to get this over with as quickly as possible.

Ike guided her into the last pew, on the aisle, where he'd be able to see everyone who came in.

People began to arrive. Middle-aged men in business

suits, some accompanied by stylishly dressed wives. A few women who looked around the same age as Mrs. Maybanks. Church acquaintances of Mrs. Maybanks, maybe, or residents in the apartment building. A group of young girls accompanied by a woman. Most likely classmates of Emily's and a teacher from her school.

The mayor appeared with an entourage. Also some men and women whose faces looked vaguely familiar to Liz. Political office holders she'd seen on TV or in the newspapers, she decided.

Mrs. Maybanks came in a side door with Kevin. Liz couldn't see her face plainly, but her hair looked as if she'd had a coif and color job that morning. Both she and Kevin walked briskly and unfalteringly.

Bruna followed with a stout, broad-faced man Liz assumed was Oleg. Mrs. Maybanks and Kevin sat in the first pew. They were joined by Dr. Ray and Attorney Schuler and two women, evidently their wives. The servants sat directly behind them.

Where was Emily?

Maybe she was with her classmates and the teacher, Liz thought. She scanned the pews. Among the school-girls she couldn't recognize one who bore the slightest resemblance to the reddish-blonde Emily she'd seen in the photo.

She turned to Ike. "I don't see Emily," she whispered.

"She's not here," he replied.

Disappointment swept over her. Until this moment she hadn't realized how much she'd counted on seeing Emily. As it stood now, she had her suspicions about her, but in order for Emily to become a full suspect, she had to see her in person, preferably close-up. She had to make a judgment of her—mostly about her ability, both mental and physical, to bludgeon her father to death.

She knew Ike had his suspicions about Emily, too, but she got the feeling he believed she was too frail to have brought a heavy bronze bookend down on her father's skull with such force. If she could only come face to face with Emily, her own instincts would tell her what this girl was capable of.

These thoughts ran through her mind throughout the service. When it was over, and the pallbearers went to bring the casket up the aisle, she felt the gentle pat of Ike's hand on her arm. "Sorry, Liz. I know you were counting on seeing her."

She nodded, knowing he thought her need to see Emily was strictly for her own satisfaction—part of the kick she got out of trying to figure out whodunit. He had no idea how much she wanted to repeat what she'd done during his last homicide case—provide him with a clue that would lead to the solution.

She watched Mrs. Maybanks and Kevin follow the casket up the aisle. Mrs. Maybanks had on a plain but chic black dress and a pearl choker. She looked relaxed. Kevin looked grim. As they passed by the pew where she and Ike were sitting, Mrs. Maybanks saw them. She smiled.

The casket was borne out the door toward a waiting hearse. The pews began to empty as people followed behind the family. Since Ike and Liz were in the last pew, they were the last to reach the door. Liz expected that Mrs. Maybanks would have gone to the crematory. Instead, she was standing in the vestibule, greeting everyone. As if this were a wedding, Liz thought. She didn't see Kevin anywhere about.

"Thank you for coming, Detective Eichle," Mrs. Maybanks said. She looked at Liz. "And thank you for coming, too. You're the young lady who was at the apartment that dreadful night, aren't you?"

"Yes." Liz felt awkward. "It was a lovely service," she said.

"Yes, it was," Mrs. Maybanks replied, with a smile.

"We noticed your daughter isn't here," Ike said.

Mrs. Maybanks gave a deep sigh. "Emily refused to come. She's such a stubborn child sometimes. We left her at home with Mariette."

Suddenly she brightened. "I've asked a few people back to the apartment for refreshments," she said. "You've both been so kind, I'd like you to join us."

Surprised as she was that Mrs. Maybanks would extend this invitation to the investigating detective and a young woman she'd seen only once, Liz's pulse quickened. She'd been given another chance to see Emily!

"Thanks," Ike said. "I have to make a stop at the station house, but I could come by afterward."

Mrs. Maybanks looked at Liz. "Do you have to go to the station house, too?"

"No," Liz replied.

"Well, then, come to the apartment in the car with

us. The detective can come later," Mrs. Maybanks said. "Kevin should be back by then. He went to the crematorium with Dr. Ray and Mr. Schuler."

She spoke brightly for a woman whose husband had just been borne off to be cremated. Liz couldn't help thinking she seemed to be enjoying the funeral. If her grief could be measured on a scale of one to ten, it might be close to zero.

Ike said he'd see them later. Mrs. Maybanks took Liz's arm, saying Oleg would be bringing the car around any minute now.

Bruna appeared. "We gonna be go to car now," she announced. She recognized Liz and smiled. "You come with us?" she asked.

"Yes—Mrs. Maybanks was kind enough to invite me," Liz replied.

Bruna nodded. "I make it plenty good food." She peered out the door. "There still be people," she said. "They wait for Madam to come out. Maybe take picture. I gonna be get you to the car quick."

This sounded as if members of the media had joined the crowd of curious onlookers, Liz thought. She was right. They stepped outside into a barrage of shouted questions and an array of cameras.

Cops kept the crowd at bay. While Bruna led the way to the waiting Lincoln town car, Liz felt a rush of anticipation. In a few minutes she'd see Emily.

But as Oleg drove the Lincoln away from the church, the thought of seeing Emily retreated to a far corner of

her mind. Anticipation gave way to a feeling, part puzzlement, part excitement. Through the car window, she
glimpsed a face in the crowd: *Yesterday's hairless goon!*

SEVEN

IKE KNEW WHAT he was talking about when he said a lot could be picked up at funerals, Liz thought, as the car headed up Park Avenue. Seeing the skinhead goon in the crowd outside the church made her suspect that he'd come there expecting to speak to Kevin after the service.

But Kevin had been whisked away to the crematory by Dr. Ray and Conrad Schuler. The skinhead must have seen Kevin leave. Why, then, did he continue to hang around till the last person, including Mrs. Maybanks, was out of the church? She couldn't think of an answer.

OLEG DROVE THE LINCOLN into the underground parking garage. They took the elevator to the lobby, where the guard recorded their names and time of arrival. The strict security measures made Liz more certain than ever that no one could enter or leave the building unnoticed. If Emily hadn't taken the bookend out in the cat carrier, then it must still be in the apartment. But why hadn't it been found? The more she asked herself that question, the more likely it seemed that Emily was the killer.

Ike would know, soon, if the police lab found any traces of human blood or hair in the carrier. And she'd know, soon, if Emily seemed strong enough to have bludgeoned her father with such force.

When they stepped off the elevator into the apartment, she remembered her blazer. "Bruna," she said. "I left my blazer in the study when I was here Friday night. Did you happen to find it?"

Bruna looked confused. "Blazer?"

"Jacket...coat...it's dark blue."

"Dark blue coat, yes," Bruna replied. "I find it this morning when I go in boss study room for make clean. Police not let nobody go in there till today. When I see coat I think it Kevin's." She scrutinized Liz and shook her head. "I not see he too big. I put in his closet. You want I get it for you, now?"

"Oh, thanks, Bruna, but I don't need you to get it now. I'll remind you about it before I leave. Okay?"

"Okay," Bruna said. "I gonna be change dress now for serve food."

As Bruna went down the kitchen corridor, a young woman wearing a white maid's uniform came out of the bedroom hallway. Slim, dark skinned, pretty, with black hair drawn back and twisted into a knot: Mariette. She didn't look more than a few years older than Emily, Liz thought. No wonder the two of them became friends.

Mrs. Maybanks saw Mariette and hastened toward

her. "How is Emily, Mariette?" Liz heard her ask. "I hope she's going to come out of her room."

"I do not think she wants to come out," Mariette replied.

"Perhaps Kevin can persuade her," Mrs. Maybanks said.

At that moment, the elevator doors slid open and several men and women stepped off. Business associates of Gregory Maybanks and their spouses, Liz decided.

Mrs. Maybanks turned and greeted them. "Thank you for attending the service," she said. "Welcome to my home."

Liz wasn't surprised when they introduced themselves to Mrs. Maybanks. Evidently she didn't know many of the people at the funeral, but invited them, anyway, just as she'd invited Ike and her. She was making up for all the years she'd been denied social contact.

Her cordiality heightened with each new group of arrivals. Liz saw her extend an especially warm welcome to the woman and the young girls Liz had seen in the church.

About ten or fifteen minutes later, the living room was thronged. She saw Kevin in the crowd. That meant he'd returned from the crematory with Dr. Ray and Mr. Schuler. They must be somewhere about, but she didn't see them. She didn't see anyone who could be Emily, either. *Why had she refused to attend the funeral, and why didn't she want to come out of her room?*

Kevin saw her and made his way to her. "Hello,"

he said, with a warm smile. "You were here the night my father…died, weren't you? You were with the other detectives."

"Yes, I was here, but I'm not a detective. I work for the Medical Examiner," she replied. She extended her hand. "My name is Liz Rooney."

He took her hand in a firm clasp. "I thought you were kind of young to be a detective," he said. "You don't look much older than my sister, Emily."

"I'd really like to meet Emily."

"She's in her room with some girls from her school. I was in there a few minutes ago, talking to them."

"Are they going to come out?"

"I think so. I told Em that Bruna made shrimp sandwiches. If that doesn't get her out here, nothing will." He paused. "Sounds like you're interested in Emily." A look of puzzlement on his face suggested he wondered why.

Liz thought fast. "Bruna told me Emily has a cat," she explained. "I'm a cat person, too."

This was not exactly true. The only cat she'd ever had a stroking relationship with was Gram's old tom, Hercules.

"Tell you what—I'll go and try to hurry her up," Kevin said.

What a nice young man, she thought, watching him go. Why did Mariette describe him to Ike as a *trompeur?* He didn't seem at all deceitful. Could she have figured that French word incorrectly?

Across the room she saw the woman she'd noticed in

the church with Emily's school friends. She appeared to be alone. Liz decided to join her. She must have an interest in Emily or she wouldn't be here. This might be a chance to get some insight into Emily's personality.

"Hello," Liz said, approaching her, introducing herself. "I noticed you were with Emily's friends. Are you one of her teachers?"

The woman, a fiftyish, beauty salon blonde, smartly dressed in a black and white print dress, and wearing a wedding band, said her name was Jane Goller and, yes, she was Emily's English teacher.

"The girls went to Emily's room," she said. She gave an impatient sigh, adding, "I have to leave in a little while and I have to see that they all get home." She said that she'd been appointed to represent the school at Gregory Maybanks's funeral and to accompany Emily's friends.

Liz decided to get right to the point. "Is Emily well liked at school?" she asked.

"Oh, yes, she has no problem making friends," Mrs. Goller replied. "Why do you ask?"

"Because I know she's been unhappy at school lately."

At that moment Mariette, and Bruna, who'd changed from her funeral attire into a gray serving uniform, entered the room and passed among the guests with trays of assorted wines in long-stemmed glasses. Liz chose one of the whites. This was definitely not from a box in the fridge, she thought, with her first taste.

Evidently Mrs. Goller agreed. She emptied her goblet

in a few gulps and reached for another from the next passing tray. "If Emily's unhappy at school, it's because she's doing poorly in all her subjects," she said.

By the time Mrs. Goller downed her second glass of this potent wine, her tongue would be loosened, Liz thought. Here was her chance to find out if Emily had shown any animosity toward her father, in school.

"I'm sorry to hear she's not doing well," she said. "But this happens, sometimes, with girls her age. It's a phase they go through. They become underachievers. As a teacher, you know that, of course."

Mrs. Goller nodded and brought the level of wine in her goblet down about two inches.

"I remember when I was thirteen," Liz continued. "My grades took a nosedive. Fortunately, my parents were very patient with me."

"Unfortunately, Emily's father was not at all patient with her," Mrs. Goller said between gulps.

Liz feigned surprise. "Oh?"

Mrs. Goller swirled the remainder of her wine around in her goblet. For a moment, Liz thought she was going to clam up, but suddenly she spoke again. "Emily is not an underachiever. She does the best she can."

Liz waited, sensing there was more to come. She was right. Mrs. Goller downed the last of her wine and went on, "Everyone at school likes Emily. She's a sweet girl. It's a shame Mr. Maybanks expected too much of her. He refused to accept the fact that her mental ability is limited. She was under terrible pressure from him, all the time. I blame him for the trouble she's in at school now—lashing out at her teachers, including me, saying she wanted to leave school and never come back. I believe the one she wanted to lash out at was her father. Poor child, she'd reached the breaking point."

Suddenly, as if she realized she'd said too much, she clapped her hand over her mouth. A moment later she said, "If you'll excuse me, I'm going to look for the powder room."

Mariette, on her way to the kitchen with a tray of empty goblets, overheard. "It is off the foyer, Madame," she said. "Right across from the elevator."

Mrs. Goller wasn't the only guest feeling the effects of Gregory Maybanks's fine wines, Liz noticed. The hushed conversations in the living room had risen to animated chatter, punctuated by occasional laughter.

Mrs. Maybanks, goblet in hand, roved about, smiling, chatting with everyone. Liz got the same feeling she had in the church. The widow was enjoying herself.

Bruna, passing by with another tray of wine, confirmed her thoughts. "Madam, she make it party," she said in a low voice.

Liz nodded. "Yes, she looks as if she's having a wonderful time."

"Is good," Bruna said. "She not have wonderful time before."

At that moment, a chime-like sound drew everyone's attention. Liz saw Mrs. Maybanks gently striking the diamond ring on her hand against her wine goblet. The stone was so large that Liz could see it plainly from across the room.

"Refreshments are being served in the dining room," Mrs. Maybanks announced.

As the guests made their way out of the living room, Liz realized she hadn't seen Ike yet. Maybe he was out in the foyer. She checked the foyer. He wasn't there. Whatever he had to attend to at the station house had taken longer than he expected.

Come to think of it, she hadn't seen Dr. Ray or Mr. Schuler yet, either. Glancing around the foyer, she saw the door to the study ajar. Maybe the doctor and the attorney were in there and Ike was with them. They wouldn't have heard Mrs. Maybanks's announcement about the refreshments. She walked to the study door, intending to go in and tell them. She was only a step away from the door, when she heard a voice.

"So, you think the boy did it, Con?"

The question startled her. She drew back to gather her wits. *Con.* That would be Conrad Schuler. He and Dr. Ray were in the study, discussing their friend's murder, and it sounded as if Schuler suspected Kevin. Was Ike with them? She peeked around the half-open door. Ike wasn't there.

Maybanks's two buddies were sitting in the same area where she'd sat the night of the murder. Along the wall behind them, she saw an open cellarette with an array of liquors. Both men held highball glasses. A whiskey bottle stood on a table between their chairs, along with a framed photograph. She couldn't see the photo plainly, but she was sure it was one she'd seen on the wall of the study that night. They'd taken it down to look at, and to talk about Maybanks and their college days.

"It all adds up, doesn't it?" Schuler said. She noticed his speech was slightly slurred. He and Dr. Ray were getting a load on while reminiscing in their old friend's study. Reminiscing and speculating about who could have killed him.

She knew she ought to leave. But if she didn't do a little spying and eavesdropping, she might miss out on something vital to the case. She was sure Dr. Ray knew all the Maybankses' family secrets and probably Schuler did, too. No sooner had this thought crossed her mind, than Dr. Ray spoke. "If I had to do it all over again, I wouldn't."

"I'm as much to blame as you," Schuler said. "We both knew it was a bizarre idea. We should have stopped it when he first started talking about it."

Dr. Ray reached for the bottle and refilled his glass. "Poor old Greg. Neither of us could imagine how it would end. But as a physician I should have known he was asking for trouble." He brushed at his eyes and took a generous quaff of whiskey.

Schuler nodded. "Setting himself up for ultimate doom."

At that moment Liz heard the sound of the elevator coming to a stop. Not wanting to be caught eavesdropping, she darted away from her vantage point. The elevator doors opened. She almost collided with Ike as he stepped off.

"What's happened, Liz?" he asked. "You look all shook up."

She replied as calmly as possible, though the impact of what she'd just overheard had set her head whirling with puzzlement. "I just heard the most incredible conversation. I don't want to discuss it here. Let's get something to eat in the dining room. I'll fill you in after we leave."

"I have something important to tell you, too," he replied. "But I agree, this is no place to discuss the case."

On the damask-draped dining room table, fine porcelain cups and saucers stood near a chased silver coffee urn. China plates were placed near an array of fancy sandwiches arranged on crystal platters. At the other end of the table, two layer cakes, one chocolate, one coconut, stood on glass pedestals, surrounded by platters of cookies in great variety and silver bowls of bonbons, mints and salted almonds.

On the massive mahogany sideboard, an assortment of wines sparkled in crystal decanters, alongside a silver tray of etched-glass goblets.

"Ike—you really should try one of the wines," Liz said as they put sandwiches on their plates.

"Good?"

"Great."

"I'll sample it after I get some food under my belt. I haven't eaten since I grabbed coffee and a doughnut around seven this morning." He dispensed coffee from the urn. "Did you get to see Emily?" he asked.

"Not yet. She's in her room with some school friends. Kevin went to get her." As she spoke, the question she'd overheard flashed back to her. In retrospect, it startled her even more. *So, you think the boy did it, Con?*

At that moment, Kevin came into the dining room with four young girls. Liz knew, instantly, which one was Emily not only because she was the only one wearing blue jeans and a white t-shirt imprinted with a likeness of Harry Potter instead of more conservative attire suitable for a funeral. She was also the only one with strawberry-blond hair, and she was almost as thin as she'd looked in the family photo.

Liz recalled Mrs. Goller saying that Emily had reached the breaking point. Well, maybe she had, and maybe she even wished her father dead, but it seemed unlikely that those thin arms, delicate wrists and small hands could have slammed a bronze bookend into his skull.

Kevin led Emily across the room. "Here she is, Em— the lady who likes cats," he said.

Liz smiled and extended her hand. "Hello, Emily— my name is Liz."

Ike thrust out his hand with a smile. "And I'm Ike."

Emily returned their smiles and shook their hands. "Hello," she said. "I want you to meet my friends."

As she introduced them, Mrs. Maybanks came hurrying to join them.

"And this is my Mom," Emily said. Liz noticed a fond look pass between them. Emily had known only coldness and cruelty from her father, but she appeared to have a bond of affection with her mother.

"I'm delighted to meet you, girls," Mrs. Maybanks said. "Please help yourselves at the table. And don't hold back. There's plenty of everything and more in the kitchen."

Emily and her friends wasted no time in filling their plates. They sat down together in a corner of the room.

"Well, I'm as hungry as a horse," Kevin said. "I'm going to hit the chow." He stepped over to the table and started filling a plate.

There was nothing about Kevin's behavior that suggested guilt, Liz noticed. His blithe, light-hearted manner was not unusual for a family member after a funeral was over. And he wasn't at all uneasy in the presence of the detective investigating his father's murder. Could she have misunderstood the meaning of Schuler's remark and misinterpreted the strange conversation between Gregory Maybanks's two old friends?

Mrs. Maybanks's voice came into her musing. "I'm glad you could come," she said to them. "You've both been so kind, and Detective Sanchez, too."

Now that she was free to socialize, Mrs. Maybanks wanted to include everyone in her new life, Liz thought.

"Lou's sorry he couldn't attend the services," Ike replied. "Somebody has to mind the store," he added with a grin.

Mrs. Maybanks excused herself to join some other people. She was having the time of her life, Liz thought, and she looked so different from the drab wraith of a woman she'd seen the night of the murder. That night her hair looked as if it hadn't seen the inside of a beauty salon in years.

"Well I'm ready for some of that chocolate cake," Ike said.

"Me, too," Liz replied.

They'd just seated themselves with their plates, when Mrs. Goller came into the dining room, looking for Emily's friends. She was expecting dinner guests and had to leave, she said. The girls must hurry and finish their food so she could take them home.

A few minutes after her friends had gone, Emily went to the table and refilled her plate. Liz called to her. "Come and sit with us, Emily."

"Okay," Emily said. She brought her plate over and sat down with them. Again, Liz checked out her wrists and hands. Again she doubted that Emily could have killed her father. She glanced at Kevin talking to some people across the room. She couldn't bring herself to believe he did it, either. But *someone* in the household was guilty. She found herself thinking about Mrs. Maybanks and the servants, again. One of them could have let the killer into the apartment from the fire stairs. But wouldn't the security guard have noticed someone entering the fire stairway? Perhaps he'd been distracted long enough for someone to have slipped in.

Ike paused between bites of cake. "I guess school will be out soon, right, Emily?" he asked.

Emily nodded. "Final exams start soon. It's a good thing they didn't start this week. I'll be out of school all this week because of my father. Kevin's been home from his school, too, but he's going back on Sunday. Did you know Kevin is going to graduate and go to Princeton?"

This was childlike prattle, Liz thought. Didn't Emily realize that the entire household was under suspicion and Kevin's college plans might have to be cancelled? Did any of them realize how serious their situation was? None of them acted as if they did. This was the strangest bunch of suspects she'd ever run up against, she decided.

She heard Ike reply to Emily. "Yes, your mother told me Kevin got into Princeton."

"Kevin's very smart, you know," Emily said.

They'd almost finished eating, when Emily looked directly at Liz. "Do you want to see my cat?" she asked.

Liz put on what she hoped was the look of a true cat fancier. "Oh, yes, Emily."

"I'm through eating. When you're finished we'll go to my room and you can see her," Emily said. She glanced at a half eaten shrimp sandwich on her plate. "I'm going to take this to Patches. She loves shrimp. She doesn't get it very often. She likes it much better than the cat food in the bags."

Liz finished eating and put her plate on a nearby serving table. "Well, I'm ready to meet your Patches," she said.

Emily looked at Ike. "Do you want to come and see my cat, too?"

"I'd like to, but I need to find Dr. Ray and talk to him for a few minutes," Ike replied.

By this time, Dr. Ray might be unable to talk, Liz thought.

"After I've seen Dr. Ray, I have to get back to the station house," Ike said. "Will you be ready to leave in about twenty minutes?"

"Sure," Liz replied. She was growing impatient to hear what Ike had to tell her, and to tell him about the strange conversation between Gregory Maybanks's two old friends.

"I'll meet you in the living room," he said.

IN EMILY'S BEDROOM, a small white cat with big green eyes and markings of tan, black and orange was curled up on the bed.

"I have a treat for you, Patches," Emily said. She placed the plate on the bed. One whiff of the shrimp, and Patches uncurled.

"She's a very pretty cat," Liz said as they watched Patches go for the shrimp. "How long have you had her?"

"Since last January, when she was a tiny little kitten. Mariette's cat had babies and she gave me one. At first my father said I couldn't keep her, but Kevin persuaded him. Kevin's very good at persuading. Did you know that Mariette was born in Haiti? That's a place down near South America. They speak French there and they have voodoo rituals. Mariette told me her grandmother was a voodoo priestess. Mariette wanted to be a voodoo priestess, too, but her family moved to the United States before she had a chance to be one."

"You're fond of Mariette, aren't you?"

Emily nodded. "Yes, she's like a big sister. She gave me a catnip mouse for Patches. It's her favorite toy." She opened a cabinet and brought out a basket of cat toys. "When Patches is finished eating, I'll show you how she loves to play with her catnip mouse."

The cabinet was the same one Kevin had opened the night of the murder, saying that Emily kept her cat stuff in there. Liz remembered how troubled he'd looked when he discovered the cat carrier was gone.

Did Emily know the carrier was now in the police lab, being tested for traces of her father's hair and blood?

Her eyes scanned the cabinet, noting the same items she'd seen there the night of the murder—an array of cat grooming equipment on the shelves, big bags of litter and cat food, and a scratching post on the floor beneath. Then she saw something she hadn't seen in the cabinet that night—a baseball bat.

"Do you play baseball, Emily?" she asked.

Emily nodded. "Softball, at school. The gym teacher takes us to the park twice a week. But athletics are over for the year now. We were supposed to clean out our gym lockers this week but I wasn't in school, so one of my friends dropped my sports stuff off yesterday. I like playing softball. I'm very good at it. The gym teacher says I pack a wallop."

Liz stared at her. If those delicate-looking arms,

wrists and hands could swing a bat so well, maybe they could have slammed the bookend into Gregory Maybanks's skull. The bat hadn't been in the cabinet until today. Ike hadn't seen it. He was unaware of Emily's ability to "pack a wallop." She wished she could go and tell him about this, right now, but she knew he was busy with the doctor and the attorney. Besides that, Emily expected her to stay and watch Patches play with the catnip mouse.

Patches devoured the shrimp sandwich, bread and all, and licked the plate clean. Then, in the manner peculiar to felines, she began to wash her face.

"Now watch this," Emily said when the grooming was finished. She tossed Patches the catnip mouse. Impatient as Liz was to talk to Ike, she had fun watching the cat cavort under the influence of catnip.

"Kevin says the smell of catnip makes Patches feel like people feel when they smoke marijuana cigarettes," Emily said. "Kevin says people smoke marijuana to feel good."

Taken by surprise, Liz couldn't come up with much of an answer. "I guess there's a similarity," she managed to say.

A glance at her watch told her it was time to meet Ike in the living room. She told Emily how much she'd enjoyed visiting with Patches, and said goodbye.

Emily smiled. "Goodbye. I'm glad you came to see Patches."

On her way down the corridor, Liz thought over Emily's remark about catnip and marijuana. Could

Kevin be into pot? She knew many kids much younger than he started experimenting with it. Maybe that was his connection to the hairless goon—the skinhead was a dealer. But why would a dealer come to the scene of the funeral? She couldn't figure that one out. She'd run this by Ike, before she told him what she'd heard while eavesdropping on Dr. Ray and Schuler. Also, she had to tell him about Emily's ability to swing a baseball bat. Then she remembered Ike had some important information for her, too. They'd have plenty to discuss.

Ike was waiting for her in the living room. They found Mrs. Maybanks and Kevin and said their good-byes.

Ike had parked his car in the underground garage. As he drove onto Park Avenue and headed downtown toward her apartment, she decided to find out what he had to tell her before she told him what she'd picked up about Emily's baseball playing and Kevin's possible pot smoking.

"What's the new development you were going to tell me about?" she asked.

"We got the results from the lab on the cat carrier," he said. "The cushion tested positive for Maybanks's hair and blood."

EIGHT

FOR A MOMENT, LIZ FELT doubly stunned. Emily's ability to pack a wallop with a baseball bat had aroused her suspicions. Now, the results of the lab test on the cat carrier strengthened them. And, not only was Emily physically able to deliver the fatal whacks, she was also clever enough to figure a way to get the murder weapon out of the apartment.

"I guess you're surprised how the tests turned out," Ike said. "I was, too."

"I would have been more surprised if I hadn't stumbled upon something," Liz replied. She told him about the bat and Emily's skill at hitting the ball.

Now it was Ike's turn to be stunned. "Well!" he said. After a few seconds he added, "there wasn't any bat in the cabinet when the room was searched."

"Emily told me the athletic program at her school ended, and one of her friends dropped off her sports things, yesterday. Does this make Emily the prime suspect?"

"It could," he replied.

He didn't want to come right out and say it, Liz thought. She understood. She'd discussed enough murder cases with Pop to know this evidence was cir-

cumstantial. Someone else could have hidden the bookend in the carrier and Emily didn't know it was in there
when she went to Mariette's apartment. The murderer
would have shoved the bookend well back, where it
wouldn't be seen right away. It wasn't heavy enough
for Emily to notice when she picked up the carrier.

But wouldn't Mariette and Emily have found it when
they took Patches out of the carrier? If so, what did they
do with it? Was Mariette protecting Emily?

"I don't know what to think," she said.

"You're not the only one," Ike replied. "We have to
handle this case with extreme care. We can't risk trau-
matizing a young girl by falsely accusing her. That's one
reason why we've been holding back on information to
the media."

"I've noticed the TV coverage has fallen off in the
last couple of days," Liz said. "And the newspapers…"
She laughed. "What a difference between this case and
the last one. No big, sensational headlines in the tabloids. Even the *National Informer* couldn't come up
with anything titillating."

"Let's hope it stays that way," Ike said. "But you
know how scandal sheets operate."

"What could they dig up about anyone in that household, Bruna and Oleg included?" she asked. "They're
not scandal sheet material."

"All they need is a suggestive headline," Ike replied.
"A question, maybe, something like 'Was Hubby Hot for
Housekeeper?' That way they wouldn't be publishing a
libelous statement, but they'd sell a lot of papers."

Liz nodded in agreement. Scandal seekers might think Maybanks and Bruna had been romantically involved and Mrs. Maybanks or Oleg had committed a crime of jealous passion. But the story below the headlines wouldn't say anything like that. It would state only that the Maybankses had a couple in their employ for many years. Anything else would be left to the readers' imaginations.

But suppose there actually was something going on between Maybanks and Bruna? She couldn't help laughing. Her mental image of this mismatched duo squashed the idea.

"So everything's on hold till you've talked with the D.A.?" she asked.

"As far as Emily is concerned, yes."

She sensed he wasn't telling her everything he suspected about Emily. Maybe after she told him what she'd overheard in the study, and how she'd seen Kevin with a character out of a gangster movie, he'd reciprocate.

Almost as if he'd read her thoughts, he said, "Didn't you say you had something important to tell me?"

"Yes, two things," she replied. First she told him about seeing Kevin with the hairless goon. "This guy wasn't the sort of person you'd expect a boy like Kevin to be hanging out with," she said. "He looked like a typical wise-guy punk. And besides being bald as a cue ball, he's a beefy, no-neck—someone I'd recognize if I ever saw him again. Well, guess what, I saw him again, hanging around outside the church after the funeral."

Ike's reactions seldom came out in his facial expressions, but she could tell by the tone of his voice that he was startled and somewhat disapproving. "Why didn't you let me know about this before?"

"I didn't think it had any bearing on the case."

"What made you change your mind?"

"Emily said something this afternoon that put a different slant on it." She repeated what Kevin had told Emily about catnip and marijuana. "This made me think Kevin might be smoking pot and the hairless goon might be his dealer. But I can't figure out why his dealer would come to the church and hang around after Kevin left for the crematory, can you?"

"I'll have to think that one over," Ike replied. "But you're right about Kevin being into marijuana. The cops found a pipe and a small amount of pot rolled up in a sock in his bureau drawer when they searched his bedroom. If it had been a sizeable amount, we would have notified the narcotics division."

"So I guess I was right. This doesn't have anything to do with the case?"

"I'm not ruling out a connection, yet. Anything else about Kevin?"

She recalled the French word Mariette had used to describe Kevin "Yes. Remember, we couldn't figure out something Mariette said in French?"

"Yeah—the word she used when she was talking about Kevin. I thought it sounded like trumpet. Did you find out what it means?"

"I think she was saying *'trompeur.'* That means deceiver."

"And the other word meant charming. Charming deceiver…" Ike reflected on this for a moment. "Mariette takes care of the family's laundry, doesn't she? She might have come across the pipe and some marijuana while putting away Kevin's clean socks. What she might have meant was Kevin isn't the perfect son he pretends to be."

Liz nodded. "That's logical."

Ike was silent for a minute. She sensed he'd latched on to a new angle.

"If this baldheaded wise guy is a dealer, there's a chance he might be pushing more than pot," he said. "Suppose Kevin got stoned on something more potent after dinner the night of the murder. What if he went into his father's study to continue the argument they'd had earlier. The argument could have turned into a fight."

She loved having him toss his ideas at her. "And Kevin, under the influence of the drug, could have picked up the bookend and bashed his father's head in."

Ike thought this over. "The idea of a drug-crazed kid losing it and attacking his father sounds plausible, but there are a couple of flaws in this scenario," he said. "First, Kevin wasn't stoned when we arrived at the apartment that night. The murder occurred in a very tight time frame. The drug wouldn't have had time to wear off."

Liz had to agree. "And besides that, what happened to the bookend?" She recalled how willing Kevin had been to have his room searched. "Well, so much for my skinhead dope dealer idea," she said.

"I'm not certain he doesn't fit into the picture some-where," Ike replied. "There's something fishy about him hanging around outside the church." He was silent for a few moments, apparently giving this some seri-ous thought. "Kevin goes back to Connecticut in a few days," he said. "If the skinhead has been selling him his marijuana, Kevin will want to take a supply back to school with him. That means they'll get together in the next couple of days. We've had all members of the Maybankses' household under surveillance since day one. I'll put the word out. When Kevin meets this wise guy and they're seen making a transaction, we'll know for sure he's a dealer. We'll have him tailed and see what shakes out."

Liz felt elated. Maybe this would turn out to be an important clue.

"You said you had something else to tell me," Ike said. "Is it about the incredible conversation you said you heard?"

"Yes. I overheard Dr. Ray and Schuler talking in the study this afternoon."

She remembered Ike had gone to the study to talk to Dr. Ray while she was with Emily and Patches. Maybe he'd picked up on something. "Before I tell what I heard, how did your talk with Dr. Ray go?" she asked.

"It didn't," he replied. "He and Schuler were loaded. I found their wives and let them know. Last I saw of them the wives were helping them board the elevator."

She sensed a note of indulgent amusement in his

voice when he added, "Were they talking loudly while you were *eavesdropping?*"

"Careful, or I won't tell you what they said."

"It's your duty as a good citizen to come forth with any information pertaining to the case."

"So now I'm a good citizen instead of an eaves-dropper?"

"I never said you couldn't be both. Come on. Tell me about this mysterious conversation between Maybanks's two old buddies."

"Okay. The first thing I heard was a question Dr. Ray asked Schuler," she said. She repeated the startling words, *"So you think the boy did it, Con?"*

Ike didn't look as impressed as she thought he would. "What was Schuler's reply?" he asked.

"He said it all added up."

"Let's hear the rest of it."

She repeated what she'd heard. She remembered it all, almost word for word, especially the parts where Dr. Ray said if he had it to do over again, he wouldn't and Schuler said he was as much to blame as Dr. Ray.

"And they mentioned something about Maybanks having a bizarre idea," she said. "The last thing I heard was Schuler saying Maybanks had set himself up for ultimate doom. What do you make of it, Ike?"

"Ultimate doom?" Ike repeated the words thought-fully. After a few moments, he nodded. "I think it might tie in with something Mrs. Maybanks said to me this afternoon. I got the feeling she didn't intend to say it—it just slipped out. That's what I wanted to talk to Dr. Ray about."

"Are you going to let me know what Mrs. Maybanks let slip?"

He hesitated. "It's just a hunch. Probably nothing to it."

"In other words, you're not going to tell me."

"There's nothing to tell yet. I'm going to give Dr. Ray time to sober up, then I'll talk to him. Probably sometime tomorrow. I'll let you know what I find out."

They were only a couple of blocks from her building. She remembered he'd said he had to go back to the station house. That meant he wouldn't come in for coffee if she suggested it. She wasn't going to get anymore information out of him tonight.

He double-parked in front of the building and walked her to the entrance.

"Thanks for taking me to the funeral," she said. "I'll be waiting to hear about your talk with Dr. Ray."

He glanced up at the Moscarettis' window. "I guess it'll be okay if I leave you at the entrance instead of seeing you to your apartment door," he said. "I just noticed one of your watchdogs looking out."

"Thanks, but it wouldn't have been necessary even if they weren't home," she said. "It's too early for prowlers to sneak in and lurk outside my door."

"Have you forgotten, not so long ago someone followed you home in broad daylight and forced his way into your apartment?" he asked.

He was referring to something that happened during

his last homicide case. Since then, Rosa and Joe had been extra vigilant.

"Who's going to follow me home, now—the hairless goon?" she asked, with a laugh. "He doesn't even know I exist."

Ike flashed a grin. "It's a good thing he doesn't." He turned to go. "I'll be tied up with the D.A. most of tomorrow morning, and I'll have my talk with Dr. Ray later in the day," he said—his way of telling her he'd be in touch with her sometime tomorrow.

It was just as well he hadn't told her what Mrs. Maybanks let slip, she thought, as she let herself into her apartment and locked it. She had enough to mull over. This case had more twists and turns to it than any she'd ever followed. She couldn't wait another minute to start reviewing today's developments.

She took her notebook out of her purse and curled up on the sofa to go over her notes and add more. After a few minutes, she began to feel uncomfortably warm and realized she still had her sweater on. As she took it off, she remembered her blue blazer was still in the Maybankses' apartment—hanging in Kevin's closet, according to Bruna. Her mind had been so full of the case, she'd forgotten it, again. Well, the weather was getting warm. She wouldn't need it tomorrow morning—or until fall, for that matter. But she'd better pick it up tomorrow, after work. She'd give Bruna a call in the morning.

The phone rang. When she picked up she heard Phil

Perillo's unmistakable voice. She knew his slight Irish accent was put on, but it always made her smile.

"Is this my favorite Colleen?"

She loved his blarney, and loved bantering with him, too. "That depends—what number are you calling?" she asked.

"The number of the prettiest Irish redhead I've ever seen," he replied.

She couldn't think of a quick, clever comeback. Instead, she laughed, saying, "Hello, Phil."

"And how are you, Liz, darlin'?"

"Great. You?"

"Fine. Counting the hours till our date Friday night."

She hadn't exactly been counting the hours. She hadn't even thought about her date with Phil since her dinner with Sophie. How could she have forgotten, even temporarily? she asked herself. The sound of his voice reminded her how attractive he was and what a wonderful time they'd had at the Rainbow Room. The Maybanks case had really taken over her mind, she decided.

"Have you been following the Gregory Maybanks murder?" he asked.

That was another plus for Phil. He didn't think there was anything abnormal about a young woman being intensely interested in homicides.

"Yes, I'm into it," she replied. "It has me baffled—but that's part of the fun of following a case."

"Friday night you can tell me what clues you've picked up," he said. "Maybe we should put our heads together and see what we can come up with." He laughed. "Matter of fact, putting our heads together for any reason sounds good to me."

"I'll bet you say that to all your Colleens," she replied.

"I swear, I've never said it before. You put such thoughts in my head, Liz, darlin'."

She almost said, "hold that thought till Friday," but decided against it. Bantering was fun, but she couldn't be sure he wouldn't take it seriously.

"What time shall I be ready on Friday?" she asked.

"I'll pick you up at seven in the limo. I've made reservations for dinner at the St. Regis."

Another princess evening, she thought, after they said goodbye. The only words she could think of to describe Phil's style were French. *Bon Vivant... Savoir Faire,* and of course the highly anglicized *Gourmet.* Besides having a zest for high life and knowing how to handle it, Phil was into good food as much as she was into homicides.

She went back to her notebook. There were several new developments to add. She jotted them down. Mrs. Maybanks turning the post-funeral reception into a lively party... Kevin's involvement with the skinhead... His pot smoking... The strange conversation between Dr. Ray and Schuler... Emily's bat-swinging ability... And the results of the police lab test on the cat carrier.

Written down, the new information about Emily seemed even more incriminating. The D.A. must be waiting for one more piece of evidence against her before he made his move.

She reviewed her notes. There was so much unexplained data. Like Ike's promise to tell her what he'd found out from Dr. Ray and Mr. Schuler. Also, something Mrs. Maybanks had inadvertently said—something Ike thought might have a connection to Schuler's statement about Maybanks setting himself up for ultimate doom.

A thought struck her. Ike seemed to think whatever Mrs. Maybanks let slip was important. Did that mean the non-grieving widow might be involved in her husband's murder?

By this time tomorrow, she'd know.

NINE

ON HER WAY TO WORK the next morning, Liz reminded herself not to put off getting her blazer. Kevin might throw it in his bag when he headed back to school, thinking it was his. If he'd had a few puffs of pot, he wouldn't even notice it was too small for him, she thought, tongue-in-cheek.

She phoned the Maybankses' apartment when she arrived at her office. Bruna answered.

"You come to apartment after you done work. I have it ready for you," she said.

Sophie phoned during the morning. They hadn't talked since their dinner together, the night she went to check out the balconies.

"What did you decide about Spider Man?" Sophie asked.

Liz told her the Spider Man angle was history. "But I picked up plenty at the funeral and afterward at the Maybankses' apartment."

"You went to their apartment? How did you manage that?"

"There was a reception after the funeral. We saw Mrs. Maybanks as we were leaving the church and she invited us."

"Can we meet for coffee after work?" Sophie asked. "I'll have to make it quick—I'm meeting Ralph for dinner. But I can't wait to hear all about the funeral and get an update on the case."

"Sure. The coffeehouse near the station at five-thirty?"

"See you there."

THEY SAT AT A TABLE in a corner. Liz made sure adjacent tables were unoccupied. They could talk without being overheard.

"So who's your prime suspect?" Sophie asked, when they were settled with their coffee.

"I wish I could make up my mind," Liz replied.

"Around the station house the odds are on Mrs. Maybanks."

"That's as good a bet as any. She certainly didn't act like a grieving widow." She told about Mrs. Maybanks appearing at the funeral sporting a fresh hair-do and color job, and how she'd enjoyed herself at the post-funeral reception. "Quoting Bruna, the housekeeper, 'Madam make it like party.'"

"Actually, it's not unusual for widows to relax after the funeral's over," Sophie said. "But I never heard of one having her hair colored for the occasion."

"I got the feeling she hadn't had such a good time in years," Liz said. "Bruna as much as said so, too."

"Bruna. How about her? Could she have done it?"

"Sure. I know she disliked Maybanks."

"And her husband, the butler or whatever he is. Wasn't he the one who discovered the body? How about him?"

"Anyone in the household could have done it," Liz said.

"Even the kids?"

"Sure. Both of them had rows with their father only a few hours before he was found murdered."

"Did you get to see the daughter at the funeral?"

"Better than that. I had close contact with her in the apartment after the funeral. She's skinny, but she must be wiry. I found out she's strong enough to have given her father a good whack." She told Sophie about the bat.

"Wow," Sophie said. "And I heard she left the apartment with her cat the night of the murder and the cat carrier was in the police lab for tests. Were the tests positive for her father's blood?"

"Yes. So we know the bookend was in the carrier at one time or another."

"Then Emily must be the prime suspect."

"Ike says she could be, but the D.A.'s holding off."

"You say both kids had rows with their father the night of the murder?"

"Yes. Mariette, the maid, overheard a heated argument in Maybanks's study just before dinner, and nobody else but Kevin could have been in there. Besides that, Oleg said Maybanks was angry with Kevin all during dinner. Kevin told Ike it was because he slacked off on his studies after he was accepted at Princeton, and his grades went down."

"And Ike didn't buy that?"

"No. It wasn't as if he'd flunked anything. He only went down to B's, and it didn't affect his Princeton acceptance. Ike was sure Maybanks wouldn't have made a big deal of it."

"So the argument had to be about something else. That might be an important factor in the case."

Liz nodded. "He probably wouldn't have lied about it if it wasn't."

"How did the kids act at the post-funeral reception?" Sophie asked.

"Emily was shy at first but she loosened up and even invited me to her room to see her cat."

"And Kevin?"

"He was the perfect host, greeting everyone, chatting with everyone. He's very charming for a kid his age." As Liz spoke, she remembered Mariette's description of Kevin. A charming deceiver. She told Sophie about it.

"Sounds like the maid doesn't trust Kevin," Sophie said. "Why?"

"Ike thinks it might be because she found marijuana in Kevin's room."

Sophie nodded. "That could be why." She laughed. "Also, that could be why Kevin is so pleasant and charming." She gave a sudden frown. "Kevin could be on something stronger than pot. Maybe he got stoned that night and lost control."

"Ike thought of that, too." Liz replied. She told Sophie about the hairless goon. "Ike thinks this skinhead guy might be Kevin's dealer. He thinks Kevin will want to get a supply of dope before he goes back to school. He's supposed to go back on Sunday."

"So the cops tail Kevin to the skinhead dealer and they put a tail on Hairless Harry after that?"

"Yes. Ike thinks he fits into the picture somewhere."

"Is there a chance this goon could have killed Maybanks?"

"No. He couldn't get in or out of the building without being seen by the guard."

"Unless the guard was diverted by an accomplice," Sophie said. She looked at her watch and sighed. "I've got to split in a minute and we haven't talked enough." Suddenly she smiled. "Your date with Phil is tomorrow night, isn't it?"

"Yes. We're going to the St. Regis."

"A limo, too, I suppose."

"Right."

"You don't sound very excited."

"I guess I'm too wrapped up in this case. But I know I'll have a wonderful time. With Phil, how else could it be?"

"I'll call you Saturday morning to hear all about it."

"By then I'll have even more to tell you about the case," Liz said.

She would, she thought, watching Sophie leave. Tonight, Ike was going to tell her what he found out when he talked to Dr. Ray. There was a good chance he'd discovered the meaning of Schuler's puzzling statement about ultimate doom, and pieced it together with what Mrs. Maybanks let slip. Again, she wondered if Mrs. Maybanks's inadvertent remark would incriminate her in the murder.

Too bad Sophie had to rush off to meet Ralph. She would have had some ideas about all this, Liz thought, as she left the coffeehouse. Well, Ike would clear up that puzzle tonight.

Meanwhile, while she was picking up her blazer at the Maybankses' apartment, maybe she'd get a few ideas of her own.

IN THE MAYBANKSES' APARTMENT, Bruna was waiting at the elevator. She handed a Sohms Fifth Avenue bag to Liz. "I put coat in here," she said. "But you not go yet, I tell Madam you gonna be come. She say you wait few minutes—she want to see you. She in the boss study room with Mr. Schuler."

Mrs. Maybanks was probably going over estate matters with the attorney, Liz thought. She glanced into the bag to make sure Bruna had put the right blazer in it. She didn't want to find one of Kevin's preppy tweeds when she got home.

"I'd like to see Mrs. Maybanks, too," she said. "But I can only stay a few minutes." She wanted to get home and wait for Ike's phone call.

"You wait here," Bruna said, motioning toward the living room. "I gonna be tell Emily you come. She be glad. She not go out of house since the boss dead."

"Why not?" Liz asked. Surely Emily wasn't being

confined to the apartment by the police. Ike would have told her.

Bruna shrugged her shoulders. "She say she not feel like go out. Emily, she funny girl sometimes." She turned toward the bedroom corridor.

Liz went into the living room and sat down on one of the handsome, tapestried chairs. Without the post-funeral crowd in the room, she was able to get a good look at the elegant furnishings. A pale blue silk damask sofa. Rose-and-blue Persian rugs. A Chinese vase filled with white roses on a mahogany grand piano. A huge mirror which looked as if it came from a French palace. A gilded cabinet full of antique bibelots. Inlaid wood tables with delicate legs. Walls hung with oil paintings in ornate frames—many of them old master originals, she was sure. Gregory Maybanks certainly didn't mind spending money. The contents of this room, alone, must be worth a cool million.

She thought of Mrs. Maybanks in the study with Schuler, finding out just how wealthy she was as Gregory Maybanks's widow. But chances were the immense fortune she'd come into would not please her as much as her new life. The gilded cage had been sprung open.

A voice came into her musings. "Good evening, Miss Rooney."

Mrs. Maybanks, looking quite attractive in a black silk suit and pearl necklace, entered the room.

Liz sprang to her feet. "Good evening, Mrs. Maybanks."

"Thank you for waiting," Mrs. Maybanks said. She

gestured for Liz to be seated, and sat down beside her on the sofa. "I wanted to thank you for being so kind to Emily yesterday. She told me what a nice visit you had."

"Yes, we did," Liz replied. "I thought I might get to see her today. Bruna went to tell her I'm here."

Mrs. Maybanks smiled. "I know she'll be glad to see you. Kevin will be, too. He should be home in a few minutes," she said. "He went out on an errand." She glanced at the small, gold watch encircling her wrist with a diamond-studded band. "It's almost time for dinner. We'd love to have you stay and eat with us, Miss Rooney."

Liz hoped her surprise was not obvious. "Thank you, but I have to get home for an important phone call," she replied. Mrs. Maybanks really needed friends, she thought. On an impulse, she added, "please call me Liz."

"I will," Mrs. Maybanks said, breaking into a smile. "And you must call me Thelma."

Liz, the cop's daughter and Thelma, the billionaire's widow. After years of social isolation, Mrs. Maybanks wanted to start making friends without delay, and never mind the disparity in age or financial status.

At that moment Emily came into the room. "Hello," she said. "I'm glad to see you. We've had lots of company today. Mr. Schuler came to see Mother this afternoon, and Mrs. Goller was here this morning."

Mrs. Goller. Liz wracked her brain. *Oh—the teacher.*

"She came to tell me everything's all right at school," Emily said. "I wasn't ever going back, you know. My father was going to make me go back and apologize to my teachers for being rude, but now he's dead and he can't make me do that, and Mrs. Goller said everyone at school understands why I was rude and I can go back on Monday and I don't have to tell anyone I'm sorry unless I want to."

"Do you want to?" Liz asked.

"I think I might," Emily replied. "They were all so nice—the teachers. They sent me cards and notes and said they wanted me to come back."

"Tell Liz what else Mrs. Goller had to say, dear," Mrs. Maybanks said.

A smile lighted Emily's face. "I don't have to be in college prep anymore."

"The school's college prep program is for students in ninth grade on, but it's open to eighth graders," Mrs. Maybanks explained. Suddenly, her eyes flashed and a torrent of words spilled from her tightened lips. "Emily never should have been in it. It was her father's idea. He insisted on it, and she's been miserable ever since. He wouldn't allow her to withdraw, even though the teachers advised it. He was in a constant battle with the school about it. Poor child, he made her life a living hell."

The outburst surprised Liz. Until now, Mrs. Maybanks always seemed so in control of her emotions.

"Doesn't the school have the final decision on something like that?" Liz asked.

Her sudden flare-up over, Mrs. Maybanks sighed

and shook her head. "Not when they're getting a big endowment from a child's father."

"My father gave the school a lot of money," Emily said. "That's why they had to do whatever he said. But now he's dead and they don't have to do that anymore."

The sudden appearance of Kevin put an end to this revealing talk. "Hi," he said, stepping into the room, looking every inch the all-American prep school lad in khaki slacks and a camel-colored sweater over a white button-down shirt. He smiled at Liz. "I didn't know you were here or I would have come home sooner."

Not many grown men had such charm, Liz thought. How did this eighteen-year-old kid acquire it? Certainly not from his father. "Hello, Kevin, it's nice to see you again," she said.

"I asked Liz to stay for dinner but she said she can't," Mrs. Maybanks said. "Maybe you can persuade her, Kevin."

"What can I do to make you say you'll stay?" Kevin asked, looking at Liz, flashing a smile.

Why weren't there guys like Kevin around when she was a teenager? Liz thought. "I wish I could stay, but I really have to get home," she said. She rose from her chair, thinking about Ike's phone call. They had plenty to discuss when he came over tonight.

Mrs. Maybanks and Emily got up, too. "Well, another time, then," Mrs. Maybanks said.

"We can have company any time we want to, now that my father is dead," Emily added.

"I'll see you to the elevator," Mrs. Maybanks said.

As they were leaving the living room, Liz heard Kevin speak to Emily.

"Have you been in the house all day again, Em? That's not good for you. It's great weather outside. Why don't you take a walk up the block and back before dinner? There's still time before Bruna calls us to the table."

His concern for Emily touched Liz. There was a bond of affection between this brother and sister. A sudden possibility struck her. Could Kevin have joined Emily in begging their father not to have her cat destroyed? Could their father's refusal have stirred the kids to such anger that they both lost control? She had a momentary imagery of Emily striking her father first, and then Kevin finishing the job. This case was making her imagination run wild, she thought.

The elevator was waiting and she got on. In the lobby, she waved at the security guard and hurried out of the building.

The doorman asked her if she wanted a cab.

"Thanks, but not this evening," she replied. The weather was so nice, she thought she'd walk to the subway.

But she'd only gone a few steps when she changed her mind. Walking to the subway, then riding to her stop would take a lot more time than hopping in a cab. She wanted to get home as soon as possible so as not to miss Ike's call.

She'd just stepped to the curb to hail a taxi when

she felt a bruising grip on her arm from behind and something metal-sharp at her ribs.

A raspy voice spoke, "Don't make no noise. Just come with me, nice and quiet, and you won't get hurt."

TEN

FEAR OVERPOWERED HER, almost cutting off her breath, propelling her heart into a rampant spin. She felt as if her whole body had turned into jelly. Even if the raspy-voiced man hadn't warned her, she didn't have the ability to scream.

Within seconds, she was shoved into the backseat of a car. She noticed dark tinted windows before the car lurched off, nearly throwing her to the floor. Indignation displaced some of her fear. She wanted to ask Raspy Voice if he'd ever heard of seatbelts, but the thought of the metal object—most certainly a knife—held back the caustic question.

Through it all, she'd managed to hang on to her purse, but the Sohms Fifth Avenue bag containing her blazer had fallen to the sidewalk and was left behind.

Still weak with terror, she tried to regain her composure. *Think,* she told herself. She was sure there were only two men involved—the driver and the one who'd forced her into the car. In her brief look at the driver she had only a glimpse of dark hair straggling from under the back of a soiled baseball cap. She didn't get a chance to see the other man. He wrapped a blindfold around her head, twisted her arms behind her back and taped her wrists together...

She took a deep, calming breath and continued to think. She knew she was being kidnapped. But the motive for kidnapping was ransom money. This happened to wealthy people. Why would anyone kidnap the daughter of a retired cop? Were these two men ex-convicts who held a grudge against Pop for helping send them to prison, and now that they were out, they wanted revenge? If they knew she was Pop's daughter, they could have been tailing her. They could have seen her go into the building and waited for her to come out.

She took another breath to steady her voice. "Would you mind telling me what this is all about?" she asked, trying to sound as if she wasn't scared out of her wits.

"Shut up," Raspy Voice snarled. Except for a trace of some foreign accent, he spoke like a character in an old Edward G. Robinson gangster movie.

"This broad don't talk like no kid," the driver said. His vernacular of the New York streets also blended with a foreign accent.

"You shut up, too," Raspy Voice retorted. "Whadda we care how she talks?"

Liz got the distinct impression that neither man was a Rhodes Scholar. They'd staged a kidnapping in broad daylight on Park Avenue. But, with no signs of a struggle, she and Raspy Voice hadn't attracted any attention. She should have screamed. She might have been rescued before he could use his knife on her.

Hoping to confirm her idea that she'd been kidnapped as a reprisal against Pop, she listened to the testy exchange between her two captors.

"Can't you go no faster?"

"Whaddaya want I should do, dumbass—grow wings?"

"If you don't step on it, we'll never get to the tunnel," Raspy Voice complained.

The tunnel? What tunnel? Were they taking her to Brooklyn? New Jersey?

Raspy Voice continued complaining. "Lotsa people musta seen me and the girl back there. If anyone figured what I done, they coulda called the cops."

"If anyone figured this was a snatch, it's your fault, dumbass. I told you we shoulda waited till dark," the driver retorted.

"Shut up. The girl wouldn't be going out alone after dark."

Curiosity overcame some of Liz's fear. "Excuse me," she said. "I really would like to know why I have been abducted."

She wasn't surprised when Raspy Voice told her to shut up.

The driver uttered a loud curse. "Wanna know what I think? We got the wrong girl."

"Shut up. She got red hair like the kid said, ain't she? And I told you I seen her leave the church with her old lady and get into the car."

Lights flashed on in Liz's mind. The man with the raspy voice was the hairless goon, and he thought she was Emily. She'd been kidnapped by mistake!

Now the ugly truth confronted her. "The kid" had to be Kevin. He must have owed the skinhead big bucks for drugs, and the only way he could raise it was to set his sister up for kidnapping. He knew his mother would pay the ransom.

She remembered Kevin reminding Emily she hadn't been out of the house for days and urging her to go for a walk before dinner. She also recalled Emily telling her that Kevin was very good at persuading. The kidnappers must have been waiting to grab the red-haired sister when she came out of the building. Reluctant as Liz was to believe that Kevin could do anything so monstrous, his guilt seemed undeniable.

It was a clever plan, except for one thing. Kevin hadn't thought about the possibility of another red-haired girl emerging from the building and being mistaken for Emily. He didn't know that the hairless guy had seen this same redhead come out of St. Bartholomew's with Mrs. Maybanks and drive off in the family Lincoln.

Should she tell these two creeps they had the wrong girl? Would they let her go if they knew she wasn't the daughter of billionaire Gregory Maybanks? Her instincts told her not to count on it.

She tried to calm her fear by telling herself this entire operation seemed amateurish. Most likely these two punks had never kidnapped anyone before. Also, they weren't very smart. But that didn't make them any less dangerous. They wanted money, and if they found out the kidnapping had been for nothing, there was no telling how they'd react. She shuddered, remembering the feel of the knife against her ribs.

The driver let loose with a string of foreign words. The way he spat them out, she knew they were curses. "You think she's the only redhead broad living in that ritzy joint?" he asked. "I tell you, we got the wrong one."

When the skinhead failed to evoke his usual "shut up," Liz knew he was giving this some serious thought. When he spoke again, he sounded apprehensive.

"If Big Tiny finds out we done a snatch job, we're dead meat. You know that's one kinda job he don't do."

Liz's ears perked. This sounded as if the driver and the skinhead were punks in a big criminal operation. They'd pulled off a kidnapping on their own, without the sanction of a boss named Big Tiny and they'd botched it.

She almost laughed, but her humorous slant was short-lived. The driver's next remark sent daggers of fear into her heart, again.

"Big Tiny not gonna find out."

There was no question as to what he meant. They'd have to kill her.

She felt mired down in terror and despair. She'd been in predicaments before, but this time she could think of no way out. She tried to bolster her spirits by telling herself she was probably safe while she was in the car. It wasn't likely the hairless guy would use his knife on her while they were on their way to the tunnel he'd mentioned before. He'd wait till they got to their destination—wherever that might be.

She didn't know which was stronger, her fear or her despair.

In her mind's eye, she saw the faces of everyone who mattered in her life. Mom and Pop, Gram, Sophie, Dan. Phil, too. She remembered their date tomorrow night. Instead of going to the St. Regis in a limo, she'd be…She shook her head, trying to rid her mind of such thoughts.

Ike's face flashed into her mind. She almost succumbed to tears when she thought how he was always reminding her of the predicaments she got herself into while trying to dig up clues in homicide cases. Well, he couldn't blame her for this one. It didn't have anything to do with Gregory Maybanks's murder.

Tears weren't going to help her get out of this, she told herself. It looked like there was no way out, but while she was still alive, there was hope.

Ike had probably phoned her by now, wanting to get together and tell her he'd talked to Dr. Ray and found out the meaning of the strange conversation between him and Schuler. He'd also said he'd tell her something Mrs. Maybanks had let slip. If she hadn't gone to the Maybankses' apartment for her blazer, she might know, by now, what it all added up to.

She thought of her blazer, lying on the sidewalk near the apartment entrance. The Sohms Fifth Avenue bag would be sure to attract someone's eye. She hoped a needy person would find it. It was a nice blazer, even if it was a veritable magnet for every piece of lint, dust and hair in its vicinity. Before she wore it, she always had to give it a good brushing.

She pictured a bag lady proudly wearing a dark blue blazer covered with lint, dust and hair. Just as she was telling herself that it wasn't likely a bag lady would be trundling her cart along Park Avenue, she heard the driver curse again.

"We being followed."

Instantly, her spirits rose. Now she remembered Ike saying he was going to have the hairless goon tailed. Had there been cops watching outside the Maybankses' apartment building? Had they seen her being pushed into a car?

She heard the hairless guy stir. He was probably looking out the rear window. "You sure? I don't see no cop car back there."

"It don't have to be no cop car, you dumbass. A gray Ford LTD been a couple cars behind us since we drove off."

The skinhead's voice took on a nervous tone. "Yeah, I see it. What we gonna do now?"

"I gonna lose that *swinya*," the driver snarled.

Liz felt the car accelerate sharply to the right. She recoiled as her body collided with her captor's. Again, she wished she were wearing a seatbelt. Under the circumstances, demanding the protection of a seatbelt would be ridiculous, she thought. Anyway, if she asked for one, the hairless guy would tell her to shut up.

The violent motion of the car and the sound of honking horns told her the driver was going fast, weaving through traffic wherever he saw the slightest break. There had to be a stoplight soon, she thought. But she knew that a high-speed chase never ended with the pursued vehicle stopping for a red light....

When she heard a police siren, she decided the driver must have gone through a stop signal and the cops' vehicle followed. Under any other circumstances being in a weaving, speeding car would have plunged her into sheer fright. Now, hearing the screech of brakes and the blare of horns, and knowing the car could end up in a collision, her fear was tempered by a sense of hope.

She had a chance now. The two punks would never reach the destination where they planned to kill her. The chase would end in one of two ways. Either the driver would stop and the punks would give themselves up, or there'd be a totaling wreck.

There was no use kidding herself. The driver was not going to stop. But if she died in the inevitable car crash, at least her body would not be found in a Dumpster.

Her two captors had gone silent. She pictured the driver recklessly maneuvering the car, and Hairless looking anxiously out the rear window at the pursuit vehicle.

Hairless broke the silence, but she couldn't quite make out what he was saying. His voice wasn't coming from beside her. He must be leaning over the front seat, talking to the driver, discussing something he didn't want her to hear.

Though he'd lowered his voice, some of what he

was saying came through to her—chilling words that brought back all her previous terror *"...dump her out..."*

If the driver made a reply, she didn't hear it. Instead, a moment later, she heard him curse, then yell. The car lurched. Screams blended with the squeal of tires and the screech of brakes, as she was thrown to the floor.

She felt the car's violent shudder. In the maelstrom of a thunderous crash, she blacked out.

ELEVEN

SHE WAS LYING ON a sandy beach. She could hear the sound of waves breaking and feel the sun warming her body. She could see gulls swooping down from blue skies.

She heard Ike's voice saying it was almost time to go. "Have you decided where you want to eat tonight?" he asked.

"You decide," she replied.

"All right—how about going to the Rainbow Room for pizza?"

"Great. I'll wear my blue blazer."

POP RAN HIS HAND OVER the tail of the winged dragon bookend. "This is very sharp," he said.

"Do you think Emily did it, Pop?"

"No. I think Big Tiny did it. Mrs. Maybanks let him into the apartment from the fire stairs."

"You're right, Frank," Ike said. "Big Tiny found out the secret that only Dr. Ray and Schuler knew."

Sophie was wearing a long, pale blue dress. She was carrying a bouquet of pink roses.

"Let me see your ring, again," she said. They both

stared admiringly at the diamond as big as a cherry tomato.

"Now that you're marrying Phil, we'll both be Mrs. Perillos," Sophie said.

The strains of "When Irish Eyes are Smiling" pealed from a church organ. She found herself standing at an altar.

"Are you ready to take this man to be your lawfully wedded husband?" the priest asked. The priest was Dan.

"Yes, I'm ready," she replied. She turned to face the bridegroom. The bridegroom was Ike.

"What are you doing here, Rooney?" he asked.

DARKNESS. THROBBING PAIN in her head and shoulder. Then, hazy light. Faraway voices. Familiar voices.

"I think she's coming to." Ike's voice.

"Can you hear me, Liz?" Sophie's voice, and then her face, blurred but unmistakable.

Liz heard her own voice. "Yes, I can hear you, Sophie." She struggled to bring her surroundings into focus and her thoughts together. Where was she? Why were small hammers pounding her head and daggers stabbing her shoulder?

Another voice. A woman's. "She knows who you are. That's good."

"Does that mean she's going to be okay, Doctor?" Ike's voice.

"It's a favorable sign. She'll have to be admitted and some tests run."

A doctor? Liz tried to put their talk together and

make some sense of it. She wanted to ask what had happened to her, but a stab of pain in her head halted her words. She must have grimaced—perhaps groaned.

"She's hurting." Sophie's voice.

"We'll give her a shot now," the doctor said. "She'll probably doze off again and drift in and out of sleep all night, but she should be fully awake sometime tomorrow."

Liz got it now. She was in a hospital Emergency Room. She felt confused. "What happened to me?" she asked.

Ike's face hovered above her. She saw a troubled look in his eyes. "You were in a car crash," he replied. "Don't you remember?"

"I don't remember going anywhere in a car." Suddenly, she felt scared. "Why can't I remember?"

She felt the clasp of his hand with hers. "It'll be okay," he said.

A sudden, mild sting on her arm told her she'd been given the pain shot.

"You'll feel better now," the doctor said.

SHE OPENED HER EYES. Hazy faces. Sophie. Mom and Pop. Gram. Ike. Why were they all in her apartment when she wasn't even out of bed yet?

"Are you awake, Liz?" Sophie's voice.

Her own voice. "Sure, I'm awake, Sophie. What's everyone doing here so early? How did you get in? Did the Moscarettis let you in?"

She'd barely finished asking the questions when she

realized she wasn't in her sofa bed in her apartment. She was propped up in a strange bed in an unfamiliar room with pale green walls.

Then she remembered the Emergency Room. "I know where I am now," she said. "I'm in a hospital. Ike said I was in a car crash, but I don't remember anything about it."

Mom's arms closed around her. "Yes, you were in a dreadful accident, dear. Thank heaven you weren't killed."

"The doctor said you'll be okay," Pop said, giving her a kiss on the cheek.

Gram followed with a hug and a kiss.

Liz looked at the three of them. It wouldn't have taken long for Gram to get here from Staten Island, but Mom and Pop had to come from Florida. Pop must have seen the question in her eyes.

"Ike called us last night," he said. "We took the first available flight."

"And he called me, too," Sophie said.

Liz looked at Ike, saying, "Thank you."

He returned the look with a smile. "We're all thankful it turned out as well as it did. When you feel up to it, I need to ask you some questions."

"I'll do the best I can, but I don't remember being in an accident, or even being in a car."

"You don't? Nothing at all?"

Liz started to shake her head. A sudden throb of pain made her grimace.

"She's in pain," Gram said. "Maybe we should let a nurse know."

"Does it hurt bad, dear?" Mom asked.

"It's not that bad." Not exactly the truth, but she was alert enough now not to want them all worrying.

"I'm going to find a nurse," Sophie said.

"The nurse will let the doctor know you're awake," Pop said.

Awake but still unable to remember being in a car, Liz thought. She searched her mind, trying to find her last recollection. She vaguely remembered being in the Maybankses' apartment and leaving the building, telling the doorman she didn't need a cab. She recalled walking a few steps away from the building. She'd had her purse slung over one shoulder and was carrying the bag with her blazer in it.

Her purse. Her ID. Her credit card. Her notebook…

"Was my purse found in the wreck?" she asked.

"Yes," Ike replied. "We turned it over to your mother."

"I have it right here with me, dear," Mom said.

"I had a Sohms Fifth Avenue bag, too, with my blazer in it."

"I have it," Ike said. "It fell to the sidewalk when you were getting into the car. The doorman saw you drop it. He picked it up and took it to the security desk. The guard gave it to me when we were there questioning the doorman."

"You questioned the doorman?" Suddenly she realized she didn't know half of what had happened. "Please fill me in," she said.

"Sorry, I guess we were all so concerned about you, nobody got around to telling you the whole story," Ike said. "You were kidnapped in front of the Maybankses' apartment building."

"Kidnapped!" It took her a few moments to get over this startling statement. "Why?"

"We're working on that," Ike replied. Something in his voice made her think he knew more than he wanted to reveal right now. She felt confident he'd tell her as soon as he could.

"You say the guard saw the whole thing?" she asked.

"Yes, but he said he didn't realize what was happening. He said it only looked like you were getting into a car with someone and accidentally dropped the bag. I have the bag with your blazer in my car. I'll give it to you when you're discharged."

Her blazer was taking on a life of its own, she thought.

"Am I going to be discharged soon?" she asked.

"Yes," Pop said. "The doctor assured us your injuries aren't severe. You were lucky, Lizzie. The two men in the car with you are dead."

"Two men." Her mind was a blank. "I need some more filling in," she said.

"You were in a car with the skinhead and another man who was driving," Ike said. "A police tail car was in pursuit when the driver spotted it and tried to lose it."

"Ike told us about the skinhead," Gram said. "It

makes my blood run cold when I think of him grabbing you off the sidewalk like that."

"So I was kidnapped," Liz said in puzzlement. "Why? And how did the police find out?"

"Like I said, we're still working on why you were kidnapped," Ike replied. Again, Liz got the feeling he knew more than he was letting on.

"The hairless guy was under surveillance," Ike continued. "The cops tailed him to the Maybankses' building and saw him meet Kevin Maybanks out front. They were parked up the block, intending to pick up the tail from there. They said he hung around for a while after Kevin went in. Then they saw a young, red-haired woman come out of the building and get into a car with him. They didn't notice anything unusual. When they followed the car, they didn't know for a few minutes that it wasn't the routine tail. They had no idea, at first, the young woman was being kidnapped or who she was."

"But they found out, soon enough," Pop said.

Ike grinned. "Yeah—when they contacted me with the details, I put it all together and knew it was you, Liz, and you were in trouble, again."

He was reminding her she'd gotten herself in yet another predicament, she thought. But this was worse than being held against her will in the apartment of a deranged woman or being followed home and threatened by a murder suspect.

Sophie came into the room with a nurse. A few moments later, a young, dark haired woman appeared. Her hospital ID badge read Sarah Mancini, MD.

While the nurse took Liz's blood pressure, the doctor

approached the bedside with a smile. "How are you feeling, Liz?"

"Okay, except for some pain and not being able to remember what happened."

"I've prescribed something for the pain," Dr. Mancini said. "As for not remembering the accident—that doesn't worry me. When you came to last night, you recognized your friend Sophie instantly."

"Why is my mind blank as far as being in the car is concerned?"

"We call that selective memory loss. Usually it's temporary."

Liz laughed. "Well, I'm glad I selected that and not something I want to remember."

The nurse gave Liz a cup of water and a pill.

"That should take care of the pain," the doctor said. "You're scheduled for some more tests later on. Meanwhile, get some rest."

"Rest!" Liz exclaimed. "I just woke up."

"I think the doctor is saying we should go," Mom said.

"Yes, in a few more minutes. I'll have the nurse remind you," Dr. Mancini said as she left.

Liz looked around at everyone. "Before you all go, please tell me what day this is and how long I've been here."

"It's Friday morning. You've been here since last night," Ike replied.

Friday. Her date with Phil Perillo.

She looked at Sophie. "I have to let Phil know what happened."

"He knows," Sophie said. "I phoned him right after Ike got in touch with me."

Liz glanced at Ike. He knew she'd recently had a date with someone who'd taken her to the Rainbow Room. She was sure he'd made the connection. He had sort of an amused, curious look on his face.

"The Rainbow Room guy?" he asked with a grin.

She nodded, feeling a trifle annoyed. It was as if she were his kid sister or something.

At that moment an aide came into the room carrying an enormous, elaborate floral arrangement in a huge white wicker basket.

Sophie laughed. "Speak of the devil."

Even before Liz read the card, she knew Sophie was right. This was Phil's style. The message on the card was pure Phil, too. *"Get well, my favorite Colleen."*

"What a gorgeous arrangement," Mom said. "Who's it from?"

"Phil Perillo. He's Sophie's fiancé's cousin," Liz replied. "I was supposed to go out with him tonight." She thrust the card into a mass of white rosebuds. "Please tell me more about the accident, Ike."

"The driver lost control of the car," he said. "It jumped the curb and slammed into a flight of concrete abutments and iron railings. Like your pop said, the two men were killed."

"Why wasn't I killed, too?"

"Apparently you were thrown to the floor when the driver slammed on the brakes and the car jumped the curb. When the car crashed, the kidnappers were right in line with one concrete abutment and an iron railing, but you were on the floor. That's what saved you."

What irony, she thought. She was on the floor because she couldn't brace herself when the car jumped the curb. By tying her hands behind her back and not putting a seatbelt around her, the skinhead had probably saved her life.

"Were you at the scene of the crash, Ike?"

"Yes. When I found out you were in the car being tailed, I joined in. I wasn't far behind the pursuit vehicle. I got to the scene seconds after the crash."

A nurse entered the room at that moment. "The doctor says if your tests come out okay you can go home tomorrow," she said. She paused. "And now, it's time for your company to go."

In the empty room, Liz collected her thoughts. She felt detached from her investigation of the Maybanks murder. What had Ike found out? What would he have told her if she'd been able to get home last night? If she hadn't been kidnapped, she'd know what Attorney Schuler meant when he said Maybanks had set himself up for ultimate doom. Also, she'd know what Dr. Ray meant when he said if he had it to do all over again, he wouldn't, and she'd know what Mrs. Maybanks had let slip.

Ike must be frustrated, too, she thought. He'd told her he hadn't ruled out the hairless goon having something to do with the Maybanks murder. Now the skinhead was dead. Whatever information Ike could have obtained from him was gone, and anything she might have picked up during the abduction lay buried deep in her subconscious.

She found herself getting drowsy. Something besides painkiller in that pill, she decided. She dozed off.

A few minutes after she wakened, the doctor came into the room.

"How are you feeling, Liz? Any recall?"

"No. I've been trying to remember being in the car, but it's still a blank."

"Don't worry about it. I've seen this go on a lot longer."

An aide came in. "Someone's here to see the patient," she said. "He was here before with the other visitors but he says he wants to talk to her alone. He's a police detective. Is it okay, Dr. Mancini?"

The doctor nodded. "It's okay with me, Tamika. How about you, Liz?"

"Sure," Liz replied. Ike had come back. Now they could talk.

When Ike came in, he said he had something to tell her about the Maybanks case before they discussed the kidnapping. She'd been too foggy, before, to wonder why he was working both cases. Now, she asked him about it.

He smiled. "When the news broke it was Frank Rooney's daughter who was snatched, everyone on the squad wanted in on it, so the lieutenant made it a precinct project."

Suddenly she realized she hadn't looked in a mirror since awakening. She must be a sorry sight. When she reached up to smooth her hair, her hands encountered a bandage swathed around her head. She frowned.

"What's the matter?" he asked.

"Nothing. I didn't know I was bandaged like this, that's all."

It bothered her, knowing she must look awful, but there was nothing she could do about it. "What do you have to tell me about the Maybanks case?" she asked.

"We went to the D.A. yesterday about Emily."

"I remember you told me you were meeting with him. What happened?"

"Not much. He's still not ready to move on her."

"So, she's been put on hold, pending more evidence?"

"Right."

She would have asked him if he intended to meet with the D.A. about Kevin, but that could wait. First, she wanted to find out about his visit with Dr. Ray.

"Did you talk to Dr. Ray yesterday?" she asked.

"I was just about to tell you about that," he replied.

A knock sounded on the door. Probably Mom and Pop and Gram, she thought. She hadn't expected them to come back until tonight.

"Come on in," she called.

Phil Perillo strode into the room, straight to her bedside, where he planted a big kiss squarely on her mouth.

"Liz, my darlin'—what happened to you?" he asked.

"All I could get out of Sophie was you'd been in a bad accident. But I heard on the news you'd been kidnapped."

He seemed so concerned about her; he didn't even notice Ike.

"That's right. It's kind of a long story," she replied. And one she didn't feel like going into at the moment. "I have a head injury but the doctor says I'll be okay. Thanks so much for the flowers, Phil. They're beautiful."

By this time Phil had noticed Ike. "Oh. Sorry for the intrusion," he said. "The nurse said it was okay to come in. I can come back later."

Apparently he thought Ike was a doctor, Liz decided. She introduced them, saying, "Ike's a police homicide detective."

The two men shook hands. Liz could not define the expression on Ike's face, but it reminded her of the way he'd looked when Phil phoned her one evening when Ike was in her apartment. Ike only heard one side of the brief conversation, but it had been enough for him to gather that the caller was a man. He'd looked partly curious, partly amused, just as he'd looked when he was here before.

Now Ike got to his feet, saying, "I should be shoving off."

"Don't go, Detective," Phil said. "I won't stay long. I just had to see how my favorite Colleen is doing."

"I should be getting back to the station house, anyway," Ike said. "I'll be in touch, Liz. If the doctor lets you go home tomorrow, I'll pick you up."

"Thanks. My folks will probably be here when I'm

discharged, though. My grandmother, too. They'll want to go to my apartment with me."

"I've already talked with your pop about it," Ike replied. "My car can handle everyone."

"I have a better plan," Phil said. "I'll arrange for a limo. That way nobody will be crowded and you'll be more comfortable, Liz, darlin'."

"Good idea," Ike said on his way to the door. He paused in the doorway to say, "I'll get back to you soon, Liz. Nice to meet you, Phil."

Liz felt a bit annoyed with Phil. His offer to take her home in a limousine seemed like a put-down. Also, that meant she wouldn't be seeing Ike tomorrow.

"A homicide detective," Phil said, sitting down in the chair Ike had just vacated. "Nice chap. I guess he's working on your kidnapping."

Liz nodded. She didn't feel like telling Phil about her involvement with Ike—if trying to solve a murder together could be called an involvement.

"I'm sorry I couldn't keep our date last night," she said. "Something came up."

"Just don't let it happen again," he replied with a laugh. "There'll be other nights, but not soon enough for me. I have to go to Los Angeles next week and I expect to be tied up out there awhile."

Liz ran her hand over her bandaged head. "I'm not fit to appear in public, anyway."

"Darlin'—you're prettier right now than any woman I've ever seen."

Just then the nurse's aide, Tamika, poked her head in

the door. "I have to take the patient down to Radiology," she said. She opened the door wide and rolled in a wheelchair.

Phil leaned over and kissed Liz firmly on the lips. "So it's goodbye for now, darlin'."

As he went out the door, Liz noticed Tamika staring after him. "Fine," she said, drawing the word out so it seemed like several syllables. "He your boyfriend?"

"No, he's just a regular friend," Liz replied.

"How about the other one?" Tamika asked.

Liz assumed she meant Ike. "He's just a friend, too."

Tamika brought the wheelchair over to the bed. "You got two hot looking men coming to visit you and you say neither of them's your boyfriend. What are you waiting for, girl?"

Liz pondered this on the way to Radiology. Hearing Phil described as hot didn't surprise her—but Ike? Well, maybe he was, in his own way.

Hot or not, she found herself wishing she'd told Phil to forget the limo—that she was going home with Ike. She would have, if Ike hadn't given in so readily.

It irked her that he'd caved in without a word of protest. It meant she wouldn't be seeing him tomorrow. His report on his meeting with Dr. Ray had been put off, indefinitely.

Suddenly, a disturbing thought plagued her. What if Ike had picked up the idea that there was something between her and Phil? What if this bothered him and he never got back to her again? Suppose he'd walked out of her hospital room and out of her life? Sure, he'd looked on with apparent cool while Phil kissed her and regaled her with blarney, but suppose this was just an act?

She told herself the notion was silly. That would mean Ike was jealous. For an instant she found herself pleased with idea of Ike being jealous of Phil, but the idea was short-lived. Ike's feelings toward her weren't the kind that evoked jealousy. A slight sense of regret came over her. Surprised, she quelled it. That bump on her head had shut off her mind to her kidnapping and accident, but it had also let in some bizarre thoughts.

When a sudden recollection struck her, she knew she hadn't seen the last of Ike. He had her blazer in his car. He'd have to drop by her apartment soon, to return it.

TWELVE

SHE'D BEEN BACK in her room for only a few minutes when an aide brought in her dinner tray. Not Tamika. She must have gone off duty. It didn't take Liz more than a minute to know if this one had seen Phil and Ike, she would have kept any thoughts about hot looking men to herself.

She eyed the dinner tray. Two slices of limp chicken. One large, peeled potato. A scattering of pallid green peas. A bowl of red Jell-O. A glass of something that looked like iced tea.

She must have seemed less than enthusiastic, because the aide paused before leaving the room. "You were out of it when the dietician took the dinner orders," she explained. Liz guessed that meant her tray had been filled with anything that happened to be standing around unclaimed.

But she was hungry. She ate it all. Her last meal had probably been the sandwich she'd grabbed for lunch, yesterday. Just as she was wishing there'd been a cookie or a piece of cake on the tray, Rosa and Joe appeared. They both swooped down on her with hugs.

"You gave us such a scare, Dearie," Rosa said. "I was worried sick when your mother phoned us. But she phoned again this afternoon and said you were going to be okay." She thrust out a white cardboard bakery box. "I brought you some pastries."

"Pastries! Just what I've been wishing for. You must be a mind reader, Rosa. Thanks."

"Your mother said you might be coming home tomorrow," Joe said.

"That's right. If the tests they ran on me this afternoon are okay."

"If you come home tomorrow I'll make you rigatoni with meatballs," Rosa said.

"That and a couple glasses of Chianti will go good," Joe added.

Liz opened the bakery box. "Ooh, cannolis!" she exclaimed with delight. "I need one right now." She passed the box toward them. "Here, have one with me."

"They're all for you, Dearie," Rosa said. "Go ahead—enjoy."

Liz was into her second cannoli when Dan came in. A broad smile spread over his face when he saw her sitting up, eating pastry.

"Lizzie! Looks like you're doing okay."

After she introduced the Moscarettis, he handed her a copy of the *Daily News*.

"I thought you might want to see this," he said.

Liz scanned the headline:

CAR CRASH FOILS
PARK AVE KIDNAPPING

A sub-headline read "2 ABDUCTORS DIE, YOUNG WOMAN VICTIM SURVIVES." Her picture appeared below.

"So I made the front page," she said. "Where did they get my photo?"

"I gave them one from our personnel files," Dan said. "Do you know, yet, why you were kidnapped?"

"Not yet." She explained her loss of memory. "Ike came to the hospital to question me, but I wasn't any help to him at all," she said.

But surely he'd done some digging beforehand, she thought. He must know more than he let on. She must not have been fully alert while he was here, or she would have asked him about it. If only Phil hadn't barged in.

Rosa cast her a worried look. "You don't remember anything about being kidnapped?"

"No, but the doctor says in most cases like this, the memory comes back after a while."

"What if it doesn't?" Joe asked. "The police will have a hard time getting to the bottom of this without your information."

Rosa shot him a disapproving look, but Liz could tell the question had occurred to Rosa, too.

Dan provided an answer. "Even if that should happen, chances are Liz's information won't be needed. I heard the kidnappers have been identified. They both have police records. The cops will put it all together. Don't worry about not being able to remember, Lizzie."

"I just feel bad that Ike came over here and I couldn't tell him anything."

"You can be sure he's on top of it. He probably knows the whole story by now and he'll let you know next time you see him."

Whenever that might be, she thought, with a sigh. She wished Phil hadn't shown up while Ike was here.

Rosa must have noticed the sigh. "I think Liz is tired. We should all clear out and let her get some rest," she said.

"That's what the doctor said," a nurse announced, entering the room. "She'll probably be having more company later on. We don't want to wear her out."

Liz thanked them all for coming. "And thanks for the cannolis, Rosa."

"Let's hope we'll see you tomorrow, Dearie," Rosa replied, giving her a farewell hug.

"Well, I don't want to see you for a while," Dan said. "No showing up at work until you feel right and the doctor says it's okay."

When they'd gone, Liz noticed the nurse reading the medical chart.

"Are you allowed to tell me how I'm doing?" she asked.

"Sure. You're doing fine."

"Will the doctor have my X-ray results soon?"

"Maybe." The nurse glanced back at the chart. "Are you having any pain?"

"No, that pill really did the job."

"Good. You can have another one if you need it."

After the nurse left, Liz thought, again, about her brief talk with Ike. He'd left her with a cliffhanger. What had he found out from Dr. Ray? Would he come back to the hospital tonight to fill her in? She grew drowsy before the previous, disturbing thoughts could recur. She dozed off.

When she opened her eyes, Mom and Pop and Gram were there.

"We're not staying long," Mom said. "We just wanted to say goodnight. We had dinner at a restaurant near here and we're going to take your grandmother back to Staten Island and spend the night there."

"We'll phone in the morning to find out if you're being discharged," Pop said. He handed her the late edition of the *New York Post,* saying, "I thought you'd get a kick out of this headline."

The headline was typical of the *Post.*

KIDNAPPED KUTIE OK

Liz laughed. She'd been reading tabloid headlines for years, but never dreamed she'd be the subject of one, and described as a "kutie."

"Well, the *Post* says I'm okay. I guess that means I'll be out of here tomorrow and back to work on Monday," she said.

Mom looked shocked. "You won't be in shape to go back to work on Monday."

Gram nodded. "Even if the doctor lets you go home tomorrow, I can't imagine she'd let you go back to work so soon. And you'll need looking after till you feel up to it. I want you to come back to Staten Island with me."

"Oh, Gram, thank you, but I'll be fine in my own place. It's not like I'll be alone, with the Moscarettis right downstairs."

Gram hesitated, then nodded. "Well, I know they'll take good care of you—you're lucky they've become such good friends."

"Liz has lots of good friends in Manhattan," Mom said. "Like that nice young detective George Eichle who was here before. He told us when she's discharged he'd take us all back to her apartment in his car."

Liz remembered Phil and the limo. "There's a new plan now," she said. "Phil Perillo is going to pick us up in a limousine."

"A limousine!" Gram exclaimed. "Who is this Phil Perillo? I don't remember you mentioning him before, Liz."

"He's the one who sent the flowers. She was supposed to go out with him tonight," Mom explained.

"Oh, the one who's a cousin of Sophie Pulaski's fiancé," Gram replied. "How long have you been seeing him, Liz?"

"Not very long."

"But long enough for him to want to take you home in a limousine," Pop said with a slight frown. "Does he know it's not just you he'll be taking home in the limo?"

"Yes, he knows you'll all be with me," she replied.

"Does your nice young cop know this Phil fellow is taking you home instead of him?" Gram wanted to know.

Liz got the feeling they all sensed competition and were rooting for Ike.

"Yes, they discussed it."

Mom looked surprised. "They know each other?"

"Yes, they met earlier today when they were both here."

She knew she'd be wasting her breath if she tried to

explain that there was no rivalry between Phil and Ike. They wouldn't understand both men were her friends— not potential lovers. They wouldn't believe that a man who sent outrageously large floral arrangements and hired limousines for her only wanted a fun dinner companion when he came to New York, nor would they believe that a homicide detective would spend his spare time with her only because she'd helped him solve murder cases in the past and he wanted her input in this one.

Tamika, Sophie, Mom and Pop, Gram. Even Dan. Everyone wanted to pair her off.

Soon after everyone left, her head began to hurt again. Her shoulder, too. She remembered the nurse saying she could have another pill if she needed it. As she was groping for the call button, a nurse appeared. A different one—not that it mattered. She looked just as nice and kind as the other one, and she was followed by an aide trundling a cart filled with medical supplies.

"I hope there's a pain pill for me on that cart," Liz said, scanning the bandages, swabs, vials and scissors.

The nurse nodded. "Yes, there is, and Dr. Mancini will be here in a few minutes to have a look at your head."

The aide gave Liz the pill.

"That should get you through the night," the nurse said.

The aide left. The doctor came in. She looked tired, Liz thought. But not too tired to give a warm smile and a pleasant greeting. "We're going to take your bandage off and see how you look under there," she said. "If it looks okay and the results from Radiology are okay, too, you'll be out of here tomorrow."

"How soon can I go back to work?"

"Don't rush it. I suggest Wednesday at the earliest—but only if you feel up to it. And I want you to see your own doctor as soon as possible."

Her own doctor. She thought immediately of Dr. Ray. He'd qualify. Her next thought was to wonder if Ike would ever let her know what he'd found out from him.

Dr. Mancini had removed the bandage. A minute or so later, she patted Liz's arm. "It's looking good. No need for another big dressing."

She took a hand mirror from the cart. "Here. Have a look if you want to."

Liz had a moment's shock. This was looking good? She hadn't expected to see bad bruising and lacerations all across her forehead, plus a five or six inch cut above her left eyebrow and signs of a shiner around her left eye.

She recalled being stitched in the E.R. "How did I get cut?" she asked.

"Glass shards," the doctor replied. "It would have been worse, but the cops said you were blindfolded with a scarf wrapped around your head and face."

More irony, Liz thought. "If the kidnapper hadn't blindfolded me I might be known forever as Scarface Liz," she joked. "Will the cut on my forehead leave a scar?"

"Only a slight one. And the sutures will dissolve, so they won't have to be removed."

The nurse was applying a light dressing when an aide came in. "Here's the report from Radiology, Dr. Mancini," she said, handing her a sheaf of papers.

The doctor perused the report, then looked at Liz with a big smile. "Good news, Liz. Your tests were okay. You can go home tomorrow."

THIRTEEN

TAMIKA WHEELED LIZ out of her room and down the corridor to the elevators. On her lap, Liz held the enormous basket of flowers Phil had sent. She'd thought of leaving it to be displayed somewhere else in the hospital, but at the last minute she decided Phil's feelings might be hurt if she didn't take it home with her.

Mom and Gram followed the wheelchair—Mom carrying the bag containing the clothes Liz had on when she was found in the wreck. She and Gram had brought in fresh clothing, including a white silk shirt, black pants and her best black sandals. They'd brought a necklace of silver beads, too. A trifle dressy for a trip home from the hospital, Liz thought, but she felt good, knowing she didn't look terrible.

Pop and Phil were waiting for them at the entrance.

"The limo's right outside," Phil said. "And so is a TV camera truck and a couple of newspaper photographers."

Somehow, the media had found out she was being discharged this morning, Liz thought. "If I'd known I was going to be on TV I'd have plastered my forehead with makeup," she joked. Well, thanks to Mom and Gram, she had on a trendy outfit.

While cameras clicked, Tamika helped her out of the wheelchair.

Liz gave her a hug. "Goodbye, Tamika."

"So long. You get better, now. See you on TV."

The limo driver opened the door and assisted Liz into the rear seat. Mom and Gram sat with her. Phil and Pop took two other seats and the enormous basket of flowers another.

During the ride to her apartment, Liz knew Phil was under scrutiny by Mom, Pop and Gram. If Phil was aware of this, it didn't appear to faze him. He kept up a steady stream of light talk mixed with blarney directed not only at her, but also at Mom and Gram. Mom had passed on her Killarney-blue eyes to her daughter and Gram had contributed hair the color of autumn leaves in the woods of Derry. With such a charming mother and grandmother, how could Liz miss being the prettiest woman outside of the Emerald Isle? Liz found herself expecting him to break into a chorus of "My Wild Irish Rose."

She couldn't tell how the blarney was going over with Mom and Gram, but for her it was starting to fray. By the time they got to her apartment she thought if she heard one more outrageous Irish compliment, she'd let loose with the wail of a banshee.

THEY WERE ALIGHTING FROM the limousine when Rosa and Joe came out of the building. A round of greetings followed. Liz was sure Rosa had watched from their front window the evening Phil took her to the Rainbow

Room in a limo, but the Moscarettis had never met him. She introduced him.

Liz wasn't sure if Rosa's approving smile was due to the flowers and the limousine or because she'd heard *Perillo* and was thinking *Italian.*

Rosa watched the limousine pull away. "You're the gentleman who took Liz out one Saturday night a couple of weeks ago, aren't you?" she asked.

"I am," Phil replied. "And I thought it only fitting that I bring my favorite girl home from the hospital in the style she deserves."

Liz was sure Rosa had been thinking *flowers, fancy car and Italian, too.* Now she was probably wondering where the Irish blarney came from. When Rosa gave a slight frown, Liz sensed she'd stacked Phil up against Ike. Like Mom, Pop and Gram, she was rooting for Dearie's nice young cop.

They all crowded into Liz's apartment. Seven people and a huge basket of flowers.

Mom insisted that Liz lie down on the couch while she and Gram fixed sandwiches for lunch. "We got some cold cuts and potato salad at the deli and there's plenty for everyone," she said.

"Thanks, but count us out," Rosa said. "I promised Liz I'd make rigatoni and meatballs for her. We got to go out to the market."

"And to the wine shop for the Chianti," Joe added.

Rosa nodded. "I'll start cooking soon as we get back. I'll be ready for an early dinner. You're all invited down to our place to eat."

"Great!" Pop said.

Liz gave her a hug. "Thanks so much, Rosa."

Mom and Gram expressed enthusiastic thanks, too.

"No need for you to go to all that trouble, Mrs. Moscaretti," Phil said. "I'll have Balducci's deliver a really *fine* Italian dinner for us, including a couple of bottles of really *good* Italian wine."

Liz stared at him. A fancy catered Italian dinner instead of Rosa's rigatoni. Pricey Italian wine instead of Joe's Chianti. Phil was doing it again. This time she spoke up. "Nice idea, Phil. Very thoughtful of you, but I'm hungry for some of Rosa's rigatoni."

"Me, too," Pop said.

"Anyway, you've done enough, getting the limousine," Gram said.

"And the flowers," Mom added.

Rosa looked pleased. "I'll call you when it's time to eat," she said. She and Joe left.

There was an awkward silence. Liz stole a glance at Phil. He looked more surprised than anything else. Apparently nobody had ever turned down one of his upgraded plans before.

Mom and Gram went behind the screen to make lunch sandwiches. Pop joined them, saying he was going to get a beer out of the fridge.

"Maybe Mr. Perillo would go for a beer, too," he said.

"Would you like a beer, Phil?" Liz asked. Before he could reply, she added, "I'm sorry, I'm fresh out of champagne, and the beer isn't even imported."

She didn't know how he would have replied. Gram

called out just then, "Who wants hot mustard on their salami?"

Pop had just come back with a can of Bud. "I do," he replied.

"Gram, I think there's some honey mustard in the fridge for mine," Liz said.

"How about you, Mr. Perillo?" Mom called.

Liz expected Phil to ask if there was any imported Gray Poupon on hand. Instead, he said he was going to run along.

"You should have this time with your family, Liz. I don't want to intrude," he said. "I'll hop a cab and go over to Ralph's place till it's time to catch the Amtrak back to Philly."

Mom and Gram rushed out from behind the screen.

"It was lovely meeting you, Mr. Perillo," Gram said.

"Yes, and thank you for being so kind to Liz," Mom added.

Pop extended his hand. "So long, Mr. Perillo."

"Thanks for everything, Phil," Liz said.

"Will you thank Mrs. Moscaretti for the dinner invitation and express my regrets?" he asked.

"Sure, Phil."

It seemed strange to have him leave without any parting blarney, Liz thought. When the door closed behind him, she knew a brief chapter of her life had closed, too. She'd have to be made of stone not to feel a small pang of regret. Having Phil in her life had been like being onstage in a lavish Broadway show. Now the final curtain had come down. It had been a memorable experience, but it was over.

"Fresh out of champagne and imported beer," Pop said, laughing. "Lizzie, I couldn't have said it better myself."

"You didn't want him to stay, did you, dear?" Mom asked.

"Of course she didn't," Gram said. "That blatherskite! If I couldn't take anymore of him at my age, how could she?"

"He *was* a show-off," Mom admitted. "But he was very generous." She glanced at the enormous basket of flowers.

"And practical, too," Liz said. "When the flowers are gone, that basket will make a dandy laundry hamper."

They were all relaxed now.

"Let's see if Lizzie's on the news," Pop said, switching on the TV.

She was. While eating salami sandwiches, they watched Liz being wheeled out of the hospital and helped into the limo. Her forehead didn't look too bad, Liz thought.

She smiled at Mom and Gram. "I looked pretty good for my TV debut," she said. "Thanks for bringing the outfit."

A complete run down on the kidnapping followed. The victim is the daughter of a retired NYPD detective. The motive is still undetermined. No ransom note or other communication was received by the victim's family or by the police.

If money wasn't the motive, what was? Liz wondered. Had Ike uncovered anything? Would he let her in on it? She didn't feel very hopeful.

Her kidnapping had all but shoved the Maybanks murder out of the news. The only mention of it stated that the D.A. had conferred with the police about arresting an unnamed suspect, but there had been no further developments. Ike had managed to tell her that much before Phil barged in.

Had Ike established a link between the two kidnappers and the Maybanks murder? Again, she got the discouraging feeling that she'd have to hear about it through the news media.

The phone rang. Pop checked the caller ID.

"No name. Private line," he said. "Do you want me to pick up, Lizzie?"

For an instant Liz felt a twinge of hope. It could be Ike on his cell phone. "Yes," she said.

Pop answered. "I'll put her on," he said. He handed her the phone. Her small ray of hope vanished when he added, "It's Mrs. Maybanks."

Through her disappointment, she saw something positive. She was starting to feel completely cut off from the murder investigation. Now she believed Mrs. Maybanks could be a link.

"Hello…" she said. Then, remembering the cordiality of their last meeting, she added, "Thelma."

"Liz, I've been so very disturbed ever since I heard about your kidnapping," Mrs. Maybanks said. "I still haven't gotten over the shock of you being snatched off the sidewalk in front of our building, right after you were here. Are you all right, my dear?"

"I'm okay, thanks, Thelma. A few cuts and bruises, that's all. How did you know I was home? Did you see me on TV?"

"No. Detective Eichle told me you were discharged from the hospital this morning. He was here, today, talking to Kevin."

How did Ike know she'd been discharged? Had he phoned the hospital? If he had, that might mean he intended to keep in touch with her, after all. This thought, plus the information that Ike had talked with Kevin today, restored her spirits.

"Emily and Kevin were both very upset when they heard what happened to you," Mrs. Maybanks said. "Especially Kevin. He feels responsible. He says he should have gone down to the lobby with you and made sure you got a cab."

Not many teenaged boys would be so solicitous, Liz thought. He certainly hadn't gotten this trait from his father.

"As soon as you're feeling better, I want you to have dinner with us," Mrs. Maybanks said. "Emily will be delighted to see you, but Kevin's leaving for school tomorrow."

Kevin was going back to Connecticut. Did that mean he was not under suspicion for the murder? Or was Ike letting him think he wasn't?

"Thanks, Thelma," she said. "I look forward to seeing you again, and Emily, too. I'm sorry I won't see

Kevin. Will you tell him I said hello and I appreciate his concern for me?"

"I will, my dear. And I'll phone you in a week or so about dinner."

Liz hung up the phone, thinking, as she had previously, that Mrs. Maybanks was starved for friendship. She felt almost guilty, knowing that she was going to use this as a means to continue her investigation into the murder.

"Thelma," Gram said. "Sounds like you and Mrs. Maybanks got pretty cozy."

"She must have taken a liking to you," Mom added.

"I think she needs friends," Liz said.

"That makes it convenient, doesn't it?" Pop asked with a grin.

She knew what the grin was about. Knowing her passion for following homicide cases, he'd figured she was going to use Mrs. Maybanks as a source of information.

She was right. He cast her a quizzical look. "Do you need Mrs. Maybanks? I thought Ike was keeping you informed about this case."

"He was, but…" She told him about Phil's ill-timed arrival in her hospital room.

Mom and Gram listened, too, as she described his visit in detail. They both shook their heads when she said she hadn't heard from Ike since.

"Sounds like your detective thinks there's something going on between you and that Perillo fellow," Gram said.

Mom nodded. "I think he's jealous."

They were echoing the same thoughts she'd had earlier.

She must straighten them out, just as she'd straightened herself out. "Ike wouldn't be jealous. He doesn't have that kind of feeling for me. We're good friends—that's all."

"Maybe that's the way Ike thought it was, until he saw Perillo," Pop said.

"He's a very handsome man," Gram said. "The minute I saw him I thought, *Errol Flynn.* Maybe you never heard of Errol, but when I was your age he was a big Hollywood star."

"I've seen him in old movies on TV," Liz replied. There *was* a slight resemblance, she thought.

"That would be enough to make George Eichle sit up and take notice," Mom said.

Liz recalled Tamika's comments about Ike and Phil. "Ike's a hot looking man, himself," she said. "He wouldn't be jealous just because Phil's so handsome."

"Him bursting into your hospital room and kissing you—that would do it," Gram concluded.

Liz couldn't hold back a sigh. Did other young women get into discussions like this with their families?

"You must be tired, dear," Mom said. "The Moscarettis should be getting home from shopping pretty soon. I'll phone them in a little while to see if they're there, and if they are, we'll go down there and let you take a nap. Gram and I can visit with Rosa while she's cooking."

"And Joe will probably have a ball game on TV," Pop added.

"All right," Liz replied. With the mystery surrounding the Maybanks case, the puzzlement of her kidnapping and the uncertainty about Ike's feelings toward her, she knew she had too much on her mind to fall asleep, but she could use the time alone to think things over.

When Mom phoned the Moscarettis, they were home.

"We won't come back till we're sure you've had a good rest," Mom said as she and Gram made her comfortable with a pillow and an afghan.

"Will you be okay, Lizzie?" Pop asked.

"I'll be fine," Liz said. Her head didn't hurt much today and her shoulder only felt sore. She hadn't needed a pain pill since yesterday, but they placed a glass of water along with a bottle of aspirin on the table next to the couch. Mom made sure the phone was within easy reach, too.

"Call if you need us," she said.

Alone in the apartment, Liz began to sort out her accumulated thoughts. With no medication clouding her mind and no distractions or interruptions, she was able to think clearly for the first time since the accident.

First, about Ike. She hoped he wasn't jealous. This could change their relationship. It could end their exchange of ideas and information concerning the Maybanks case and all Ike's future homicide cases.

But she wouldn't be cut off, entirely, from this case. If she encouraged Mrs. Maybanks's need for friendship, there was no telling what she could come up with on her own.

She knew she was kidding herself. Investigating Gregory Maybanks's murder was only part of it. Of far greater concern was the disheartening thought that Ike might not contact her again. She wasn't sure if his feelings had gone beyond close friendship, but in her mind, unbefuddled by pain pills, she knew hers had.

Whatever his feelings, and with or without their teamwork in homicide cases, she wanted him in her life.

Suddenly she remembered her blazer. He said he'd return it to her. He knew she was home from the hospital. Maybe he'd drop in tomorrow. If he did, she'd straighten him out about Phil. They'd soon be back on their old footing. Well, not exactly. She'd be aware of her changed feelings, and wondering if his had changed, too.

If only her head had been this clear when he was in her hospital room. She would have insisted he stay. She would have told Phil to go. She would have gotten straight answers to her questions. When she asked him if he knew why she was kidnapped, she wouldn't have let him get away with just saying they were working on it. He had to know *something*.

It was too much of a coincidence that a goon with connections to Kevin Maybanks had snatched her off the sidewalk right in front of the Maybankses' apartment. And it had happened soon after Kevin came home—from an errand, his mother said. Meanwhile, the hairless thug and the driver were in a car, waiting for her outside the building. Why?

A startling idea struck her. If Kevin owed the hairless goon a lot of money for drugs, and the goon was part of a drug operation, maybe Kevin was being threatened. Maybe he was desperate and got the idea of having Emily kidnapped for ransom. He knew their mother would shell out whatever it took for Emily's safe return. The more she thought about it, the more sense this idea made.

He must have described Emily to Hairless, who'd gone to the church to make sure he knew what she looked like. He'd hung around till he saw the family come out. He'd seen an older woman and a slim, red-haired girl get into the family car. She and Emily were the same height and build and at a distance, the ten years difference in their ages wouldn't have been noticeable. The goon assumed the women were Kevin's mother and sister.

But why would the kidnappers believe that Emily would be coming out of the building soon after Kevin went in? She tried to recall the minutes before she left the Maybankses' apartment. Had there been any talk of Emily going out? All she could remember about those last minutes was saying goodbye and getting on the elevator.

Another thing—the TV newscaster had said there'd been no communication from the kidnappers. That, too, could be explained. If a ransom note had been sent to Mrs. Maybanks beforehand, Kevin could have watched the mail and intercepted it after he found out the kidnapping had been botched. And, because the kidnappers had died before they had a chance to make the phone call, Mrs. Maybanks didn't know Emily was an intended victim. Now, with the skinhead dead, Kevin might be off the money hook.

These suppositions were logical enough to leave her with a feeling of relief. Relief soon turned to drowsiness. She fell asleep.

FOURTEEN

WHEN SHE LOOKED UP and saw Pop, she knew she'd been asleep. Mental gymnastics, she thought. She'd really given her mind a workout.

"Did I wake you up, Lizzie?"

"No, I didn't even hear you come in. How long have you been here?"

"Only a few minutes."

"I guess I was ready to wake up. What time is it?"

"Almost three. Your mother sent me up to see how you're doing. She said to bring you down there if you feel up to it."

"Three o'clock. Wow. I had a long nap. But guess what, Pop—before I fell asleep I figured out why I was kidnapped and who planned it."

"Did you, now!" Pop sat down on the edge of the couch. "So who's the guilty party?"

"It's Kevin. Don't laugh, Pop. Listen to this." In full detail, she told him how she'd arrived at her conclusion.

Pop gave an indulgent smile. "So you think Emily was supposed to be kidnapped but they got you by mistake? I don't know, Lizzie. Setting up his own sister for kidnapping because he was into a dealer for drugs? I haven't been following the case very closely, but I got the impression the boy was a straight arrow—honor student—headed for Princeton—all that."

"I know. Everyone thought he was a model son—especially his father."

"You think he owed big bucks to a drug dealer for marijuana?" Pop shook his head. "A rich kid like Kevin gets a pretty hefty spending allowance. He'd have to buy a hell of a lot of pot to get in debt. Maybe he's on the hard stuff."

"Maybe. If he is, don't you agree this might be a motive for the kidnapping?"

Pop nodded. "I have to agree, it's possible."

Discussing her kidnapping with Pop was next best to talking about it with Ike, Liz thought. Would she ever get the chance to tell Ike what she'd just told Pop? Suppressing a sigh, she glanced at the clock on the wall.

"Mom and Gram will be wondering about me. Guess I better pull myself together and go downstairs with you."

IN THE MOSCARETTIS' KITCHEN, Liz found Mom and Rosa putting together an antipasto of anchovies, ripe olives, lettuce, Italian peppers, tomatoes, onions and provolone. On the stove, a caldron of sauce bubbled like a mini-volcano.

Joe was watching TV in the living room. Gram was setting the table in the dining room. Liz noticed Rosa had brought out what must be her best tablecloth, but mindful of pasta sauce's errant ways, she'd covered it with clear plastic. The table was set with the long-stemmed, crystal wine glasses and the gold-rimmed china always displayed in an oak, glass-door cabinet, instead of the multi-colored everyday dishes and sturdy glass goblets Rosa kept on her kitchen shelves.

"It looks like a party, Rosa," Liz said.

"That's what it is, Dearie—a welcome home party, for you."

The phone on the kitchen wall rang. Rosa picked up.

"Hello… Oh, hello, Sophie… Yes, she's here. Hold on."

She handed the phone to Liz, saying, "Sophie tried to get you and when nobody answered she figured you were here." She cleared away some jars and bowls on the kitchen table. "Sit down and talk, Dearie."

Sophie said she was calling on her personal cell phone while she and her partner stopped for a coffee break. "So this will have to be quick," she said. "Ralph phoned me a few minutes ago. What happened with you and Phil?"

Not an easy question to answer, Liz thought. How could she explain that she'd discovered the prince was actually a frog? "Why do you think something happened?" she asked, playing for time to get the right words together.

"Well, Ralph's off today, and he said Phil turned up at his place around noon. He said he was going back to Philadelphia earlier than he'd planned to. Ralph knew Phil was going to pick you up at the hospital today in a limo, and planned to spend the day and evening with you."

"Phil picked me up in the limo and brought me home, but he didn't stay long."

"Ralph said Phil clammed up when he asked him why he was leaving so early. What happened?"

"He brought my parents and grandmother back to my apartment in the limo, too. I guess he realized I don't get to see them often, so that's why he didn't stay. He said he didn't want to intrude in our time together."

"That doesn't sound like Phil," Sophie said. "I'm surprised he didn't insist on taking you all to lunch at some five-star restaurant and to dinner at some ritzy hotel." She paused. "Well, I gotta go, Liz. I want to hear more about this Phil situation. I'll phone you when I'm off work."

"I couldn't help overhearing," Mom said as Liz hung up the phone. "I guess with Sophie being engaged to Ralph Perillo, she'd like it if you got involved with his cousin."

"Doesn't Sophie know about your detective?" Rosa asked.

"Sure, she knows him from the station house. She knows he and I are good friends." She hoped this wasn't going to be the topic of conversation for the rest of the day.

Pop must have sensed her feelings. "Does Sophie still want to be a homicide detective?" he asked, changing the subject.

Liz shot him a grateful look. "Yes, as soon as she's eligible, she's going to apply for detective training.

She'll make a great detective. She's very good at figuring things out."

"You're good at that, too, Liz," Gram said, coming into the kitchen from the dining room.

"Too bad she has no interest in following in her old man's footsteps," Pop said. "But I remember she and Sophie used to talk about going into business together as private investigators."

"We still talk about it once in a while," Liz replied.

Joe had come into the kitchen and caught the conversation. "If you ask me, they could use a couple of good P.I.'s on the Maybanks murder case," he said. "A house full of suspects and the police haven't even made an arrest yet."

Rosa, giving the pasta sauce a stir, nodded her head. "If I was Mrs. Maybanks, I'd be very annoyed."

"Mrs. Maybanks could be the one who did it," Gram said.

Liz was pleased when a lively discussion followed about the murder suspects. It carried over while Rosa and Mom put the food on the table, and continued during the meal. After a round or two of Chianti, it escalated into a debate.

Gram didn't know how mean a man Maybanks was, yet she insisted Mrs. Maybanks had done it. She had the most to gain by his death. All that money.

Rosa suspected Bruna and Oleg. They were foreigners, weren't they?—not American citizens. Some of those people you couldn't trust.

Even though Mom didn't know about Emily's baseball bat and the cat carrier tests, she believed Emily was guilty. "Your father always said the least likely one sometimes turns out to be the killer. Isn't that right, Frank?"

"Right," Pop said with a wink at Liz.

Did the wink mean Pop, too, thought Emily had done it? Before Liz could catch his eye again and try to interpret what the wink might have meant, Joe spoke up, "I think the daughter and the son were in cahoots and bumped off their old man, together. I saw something on TV the other night, very similar."

"I watched that with you, Joe and you're crazy, it wasn't similar at all," Rosa said. "Those kids on TV had a mean father who used to beat them and their mother."

Gregory Maybanks's pride and affection for his son was too great for him to have mistreated him in any way, Liz decided. But he regularly abused his wife and daughter in nonphysical ways. If anyone had joined with Emily in killing him, it would have been Mrs. Maybanks, not Kevin. One more possibility to discuss with Ike, if she ever got the chance.

AFTER LIZ WENT UP to her apartment with Mom, Pop and Gram, it was time to say goodbye. Her parents were going to spend the night with Gram on Staten Island and take an early flight back to Florida in the morning.

They'd been gone about half an hour when Sophie phoned again. "I'm at Ralph's place," she said. "We just finished eating Chinese takeout and we were thinking about coming over to see you."

"Great. Come on over. My folks left a little while ago and I'm feeling kind of lonesome."

She knew they wanted to find out why Phil took off in such a hurry. They sensed the potential romance was defunct. How could she tell Ralph that his cousin was…? She searched her mind for words that best described Phil, and came up with three: ostentatious, grandiloquent and insensitive.

THE MINUTE SOPHIE and Ralph walked into the apartment, Ralph noticed the basket of flowers.

"Guess I don't have to ask who gave you that," he said.

Liz smiled. "It's lovely, isn't it?"

"Must have cost a bundle," Ralph replied. "So, how are you feeling, Liz?"

"Okay. The doctor says I can go back to work on Wednesday."

"Let's get to the point," Sophie said. "We're curious about what happened with Phil."

Liz looked at Ralph. "Did he tell you Rosa and Joe Moscaretti invited us all for dinner?"

Ralph shook his head. "No. He didn't say much of anything. Only that your folks were there and he felt like he was intruding."

Did Ralph think they'd made Phil feel unwelcome? Liz felt her temper stir. "I think he felt more like rigatoni with the Moscarettis wasn't up to his gourmet dining standards," she said.

Sophie gave a sigh. "Oh, dear. We were afraid it was something like that."

Ralph frowned. "Instead of pasta with Rosa and Joe, did he want to take everybody out to a fancy restaurant?"

Liz got the feeling it wasn't the first time Phil had pulled something like this. She described what had happened. "I guess he got my Irish up," she said. She told them the remark she'd made about champagne and imported beer.

Ralph laughed. "Good for you, Liz. It's time someone got it across to Phil that he comes on too strong with everything. I tried to tell him a couple of times, but he wouldn't listen."

"I'm sure he didn't realize he might be hurting the Moscarettis' feelings," Liz said.

Sophie nodded. "That's the problem. He gets so carried away with his grandiose plans he doesn't stop to think."

"Phil makes a good first impression but he doesn't wear well," Ralph said. "I'm not surprised it's over with you two."

Liz sighed with relief. "I thought you'd be mad at me."

Sophie gave her a hug. "No use pretending we weren't hoping you and Phil would get together. But I should have known better. You've been my best friend since first grade. I know what you go for in a guy and what you don't."

"You do?" Liz asked with a laugh. "That's something I've never been sure of myself."

Not until recently, she thought. It had taken her a long time to admit she could go for Ike. Suddenly, her need to see him burst into the forefront of her emotions. Discussing the case with him was secondary. He had to return her blazer, but after that... A pang of uncertainty touched her heart.

With a shake of her head, she glanced toward the kitchenette. "You guys want something to drink? Soda? Beer? Coffee?"

"I'll have a beer as long as it's not imported," Ralph said with a wry smile. "Mind if I turn the TV on, Liz?"

"Go ahead. The remote's on the table next to the sofa."

Sophie followed Liz behind the screen. "There's something I need to tell you," she said.

"What?" Liz asked, taking a bottle of Bud out of the fridge. "Do you want beer, too, Sophie?"

"I'll have a Coke. Are you going to listen to me?"

Liz took two Cokes out. "Sure. Let's hear it."

Sophie lowered her voice. "You know I was in the Emergency Room with Ike when you came to."

"Right. I remember seeing you both when I opened my eyes. What's this all about?"

"Something happened before you regained consciousness. I thought you should know."

"Stop being so mysterious. What happened?"

"Ike kissed you."

Liz stared at her in disbelief.

"It's true. He stroked your hair and planted a kiss on your forehead, and then he took your hand and kissed it. He didn't say a word, but if you could have seen his face… Liz, I think he's in love with you."

FIFTEEN

LIZ HAD TROUBLE getting to sleep that night.

Sophie's words sounded, over and over, in her mind. She'd been too stunned by them, at first, to say anything except, "Oh?" Now, as the clock on the wall ticked away the hours, she still couldn't believe what she'd heard.

"Is that all you're going to say?" Sophie had asked. "Maybe I shouldn't have told you."

"I'm glad you told me. I'm just very surprised."

"Pleasantly?"

"Of course, pleasantly."

"Do you want to talk about it?"

Liz nodded. Surprised didn't come close to describing her feelings. Along with being stunned, she felt a high level of excitement.

Ralph's voice sounded from the other side of the screen. "What are you doing back there—brewing my beer from scratch?"

"Coming right up," Sophie called. To Liz, she whispered, "We'll have to put this on hold."

They joined Ralph and watched most of a Clint Eastwood movie. Liz thrust Sophie's startling revelation into the back of her mind. It kept working its way to the forefront. She struggled to keep it from bursting out. She couldn't allow this to overpower her thoughts. She wanted to talk about this with Sophie, but with Ralph here, she couldn't. As Sophie said, it had to be put on hold. She willed herself to concentrate on the movie.

When it ended, she switched over to the news channel.

"And now, a late breaking bulletin concerning the Park Avenue kidnapping," a newscaster was saying.

If anything could get her mind off what happened in the Emergency Room, this was it, Liz thought.

"Police announced tonight that the two men who kidnapped a retired NYPD detective's daughter last Thursday had connections to alleged racketeer Boris 'Big Tiny' Tynkov," the newscaster said. "During interrogation Tynkov admitted the two men were members of his bowling and billiards club, but denied any knowledge of the kidnapping. Police stated he's still under investigation."

A shot came on of a bulbous-faced man with thick, graying hair and dark, bushy eyebrows that accentuated his glowering expression. Racketeer Boris Tynkov.

"I do not do kidnappings," he stated, sounding like a movie actor playing Josef Stalin. "But if I did I would not be so crazy and kidnap a policeman's daughter. The two men who did this, they should be thankful they are dead."

"I wonder what he meant by that," Ralph said with a grin.

"I think he's telling the truth," Sophie said. "Big Tiny's strictly into gambling and loan sharking."

Gambling. Loan sharking. Liz's senses went on alert. What if the hairless goon wasn't a drug dealer, but, instead, a collections agent for Big Tiny? What if Kevin had racked up huge gambling losses and borrowed from the organization to repay, but the interest was so high he couldn't get out from under? This would tie in with her previous idea, that Kevin had been threatened and was desperate for money. This new angle reinforced her belief that Kevin had planned the kidnapping.

She didn't know which was the stronger—her need to see Ike and talk to him about this or her need to just see him. If she'd been able to come up with this angle, then surely he had, too. She closed her eyes, as if that would shut away the thought that Kevin might be arrested without Ike telling her it was going to happen.

"Looks like Liz is falling asleep," Sophie said. "We better go and let her get to bed."

Now, as Liz lay in bed, listening to the ticking of the clock, she didn't think she'd ever get to sleep. Thoughts of her kidnapping and of Gregory Maybanks's murder whirled around in her mind like a mental image of a three-ring circus.

When she tried to get to sleep by cutting off these thoughts, they were replaced by thoughts of Ike. Her last waking imageries were of Ike kissing her forehead and hand, and Sophie saying, "Liz, I think he's in love with you."

A KNOCK AT THE DOOR woke her up. It was light. The clock on the wall said quarter of nine. Just as last night's thoughts sprang into her mind, she heard Rosa's voice.

"I brought you some breakfast and the Sunday paper, Dearie. I have my key. I'll let myself in."

The aroma of coffee filled the apartment. Rosa put a tray on the table next to the couch and set the *New York Times* on the sofa bed. The newspaper was still neatly folded.

"Thanks so much, Rosa. But you haven't even looked at the paper yet."

"Joe's still reading the *News,* and then we're going to mass," Rosa replied. "We're in no hurry for it."

"I can't believe I slept so late," Liz said. *How could she have slept at all with her mind in such turmoil?*

"At first we were worried when we didn't hear any sounds up here, but I said to Joe, 'She's exhausted from yesterday. I'll take her some breakfast.' Are you feeling better today, Dearie?"

Liz realized she did feel better. Only some soreness from the bruises on her shoulder and head. "Yes, much better, thanks. I really appreciate the room service." *Could Sophie have been mistaken about what she saw in the Emergency Room?*

Rosa glanced at the tray. "It's just coffee and juice and a sweet roll."

"It's more than enough. You're so good to me, Rosa." *If Sophie were right, why hadn't Ike contacted her yesterday?*

"I'd do the same for my own daughter if she was here instead of way off in California," Rosa said. She headed for the door, saying, "I'll see you later, Dearie."

LIZ KEPT THE TV TURNED ON to the news channel all day. This and the *Times* would bring her up to date on the progress of the murder investigation.

But coverage of Gregory Maybanks's murder was both disappointing and puzzling. Nothing new in the paper or on television. Nothing new about her kidnapping, either. She felt like calling the TV channel and blurting out everything she believed.

Gram phoned to see how she felt and to tell her not to go back to work too soon.

Rosa came to retrieve the breakfast tray and to bring her a sandwich for lunch. "We want you to eat with us tonight," she said. "I'm making veal Parmesan. Come down at five o'clock."

After she got back from dinner with the Moscarettis, Mom and Pop phoned. Afterward, she turned on her TV again to see if she'd missed anything about her kidnapping. She hadn't. Again, she felt sure that if she'd been able to figure out Kevin's involvement, then Ike had, too.

Her need to talk this over with Ike rose to new heights. But suddenly, instead of wishing he'd phone or drop by, she found herself hoping he wouldn't—at least not tonight. She needed time to get used to the idea that his feelings for her might be more than close friendship. And she needed time to sort out her own feelings.

He must realize Sophie had noticed him kissing her forehead and hand. He must know Sophie had told her. Did he wish he hadn't done this? Was this why he hadn't been in touch?

No, she decided. It hadn't kept him from offering to drive her home from the hospital. It wasn't until after Phil barged into her room that he stopped communicating.

She began to feel caged in by these thoughts. She must break out and think of other things. Like what she was going to do tomorrow. It had to be something more than staying in her apartment and letting her mind wander into disturbing areas.

First thing in the morning, she'd call Dr. Ray's office for an appointment. Maybe he could see her tomorrow or Tuesday. She knew Dan wouldn't approve of her returning to work until she had a clean bill of health. She wanted to go back on Wednesday. She couldn't stand much more of this sitting around and speculating.

She had trouble falling asleep again that night. She'd just started to feel drowsy when another disturbing thought stole into her mind: suppose Dr. Ray was able to see her tomorrow and Ike dropped by to return her blazer while she was out. He'd leave it with the Moscarettis.

Until that moment she hadn't realized how much she'd been counting on the return of the blazer as a means to see Ike again. But she couldn't hang around her apartment day after day on the chance that he might drop by.

If only Phil hadn't interrupted her talk with Ike. If only Sophie hadn't told her what happened in the E.R. If only she could turn off these thoughts and go to sleep.

Somehow, she did.

SIXTEEN

SHE WAKENED BEFORE seven with the night's thoughts still on her mind. When she turned the TV on, a newscaster was reviewing the kidnapping, including an update on the condition of the victim. She'd been discharged from the hospital with multiple lacerations, bruises and amnesia, he said. She was unable to recall anything about the abduction or the car crash.

No mention that her memory loss was temporary.

By the time she'd showered and dressed, Rosa was at the door with breakfast.

"We heard you in the bathroom early, Dearie. That means you feel better."

"Yes. I'm mending fast." She didn't tell Rosa she was going to try and get a doctor's appointment today. Rosa would object. *"It's too soon for you to be going out, Dearie."* If Dr. Ray could see her today, she'd take a cab to his office. On her way out, she'd return the breakfast tray, let Rosa know where she was headed, and go.

She phoned Dr. Ray's office at half-past-eight on the chance that his nurse would be there. He might even be there himself. He seemed like the kind of doctor who got into the office early.

"Elizabeth Rooney!" the nurse exclaimed. "We were worried about you. We heard about your kidnapping and the car wreck. And you were injured. How are you feeling?"

"I'm doing okay, thanks, but…"

"I know—you want Dr. Ray to be sure everything's all right," the nurse said. "If you can hold, I'll speak to the doctor. Under the circumstances he might be able to squeeze you in sometime today."

This was her fifteen minutes of fame paying off, Liz thought.

The nurse's voice came on again. "Elizabeth, the doctor says if you can get over here by half-past-nine, he can see you."

On her way out, she knocked on the Moscarettis' door.

Rosa answered. She looked disapproving when she noticed Liz had her purse and was obviously going out.

"I'm returning your tray and dishes, Rosa. Thanks for taking such good care of me," Liz said. "I'm on my way to a doctor's appointment now."

"You shouldn't be going out by yourself," Rosa said, just as Liz knew she would. "If you can wait a few minutes, I'll go with you."

"Thanks, Rosa, but I'm running late. I'll be okay. I'll get a cab out front."

Before Rosa could say she shouldn't be out on the street looking for a cab all by herself, and before she could call Joe, Liz made her getaway.

The doctor's nurse greeted her with a warm smile.

"Oh, my goodness," she said, looking at Liz's cuts and bruises. "Are you still hurting?"

"Just sore," Liz replied. "It looks worse than it really is. I didn't put any makeup over the bruises. I thought the doctor might want to look at them."

"Good thinking," the nurse said. "He's with a patient now—another off-schedule appointment. The doctor got here extra early for it. He was pretty sure it wouldn't take long and he could squeeze you in."

As she spoke, the door to the doctor's consulting room opened. Liz was startled when Kevin Maybanks came out.

He seemed just as startled as she. Caught off guard, he stared at her before he pulled himself together and flashed her one of his winning smiles. "I was shocked when I heard what happened to you," he said. "I'm glad you weren't hurt bad, but it's a real bummer the car crash left you with partial amnesia. I heard on the news you can't remember anything about the kidnapping or the accident."

"That's right," she replied. "I vaguely remember being in your apartment and talking with you and your mother and Emily, but after that most everything's a blank."

"I should have gone down to the street with you and made sure you got a cab, then it would never have happened," he said.

How gallant of him, she thought, suppressing a wry smile. Mariette had described him perfectly. He was a charming deceiver—a real con artist.

She knew he was congratulating himself on his good luck. He believed there was no way anyone could connect him to the kidnapping. With the two thugs dead and she unable to remember anything they said which could incriminate him, he thought he was safe. He didn't know her memory loss was temporary. And most important of all, he didn't know her memory loss hadn't kept her from figuring out who'd planned the kidnapping.

"I'm surprised to see you here, Kevin," she said. "I thought you'd be back at school by now. When your mother phoned me Saturday she said you were leaving yesterday."

"That was the plan, but I woke up yesterday feeling rotten. Chills and fever and aches all over. I thought it might go away and I could hit the road, but it didn't, so last night my mom called Uncle Elliott—Dr. Ray—and he said for me take aspirin and come in early today, before any other patients. Oleg drove me here and the doc gave me a shot and some antibiotics and told me to go home and hit the sack."

"I guess you won't be going back to school for a few days," she said. *Before those few days were up, Ike might arrest him for planning her kidnapping.*

"The doc said I could go back in a couple of days if my temperature's down," Kevin said. He turned toward the entrance. "Well, I'd better go. Oleg's waiting. Nice to see you again. I hope you heal up soon." He flashed her another smile.

How could a child, raised in the environment Gregory Maybanks had provided for his son, grow up to be a con artist? she wondered. How could he have gambled away every cent his indulgent father gave him, and fallen prey to a loan shark? And especially, how could he have planned the kidnapping of the sister he seemed so fond of, in order to pay his gambling debt?

"So long, Kevin," she said. She didn't tell him she hoped he'd feel better soon. He deserved to feel miserable.

A few minutes later the nurse told her the doctor was ready for her.

"I didn't think I'd see you again so soon, Elizabeth," Dr. Ray said. He glanced at her forehead. "Looks like this could have been much worse. You were lucky."

"Thank you for seeing me on such short notice," Liz replied. "I want to go back to work on Wednesday."

"Well, let's have a look," he said, leading the way into his examining room. "I guess the hospital took pictures and you checked out okay. Are you still having pain?"

"No. My shoulder and forehead feel sore, that's all. And I can't remember anything about being kidnapped or the car crash. The doctor at the hospital said it's probably temporary."

He nodded. "Generally, the memory comes back."

"Well, I wouldn't mind if mine didn't," she said. "I don't want to remember that frightening experience. And the police don't need any information I could give them. They know the identity of the kidnappers."

Dr. Ray removed the dressing from her cut. "This is healing nicely," he said. He applied another patch, saying, "But last I heard, the police don't know the motive for the kidnapping. Your family never got any communication from them, did they?"

"No. But I'm sure the police have put it all together by this time. They just haven't released the information yet." *Why hadn't they? Why hadn't Kevin been arrested?*

"I guess so," the doctor replied. She noticed a troubled look cross his face.

A sudden thought hit her. Maybe Dr. Ray also thought Kevin had something to do with her kidnapping. She already knew he and Schuler suspected Kevin of the murder. She recalled the incriminating question. *"So you think the boy did it, Con?"*

A restless feeling came over her—the feeling she always got when she was on the fringes of an important clue. She had to find out what Dr. Ray had told Ike during their talk last Thursday. Instinct told her the murder was connected to something Dr. Ray and Schuler knew about Gregory Maybanks. That secret was the key to the entire case. Ike must know what it was. She didn't feel comfortable with the idea of asking the doctor about the secret. The only way she could find out was from Ike, when he returned her blazer.

"Everything looks fine, Elizabeth," the doctor said. "No reason you can't go back to work on Wednesday."

Good, she thought. Now she could hurry home. She

didn't even want to think about what she'd do if Ike had been there during her absence and left the blazer with the Moscarettis.

WHEN ROSA HEARD HER enter the building, she came out of her apartment. But she only wanted to make sure everything went okay at the doctor's. Ike hadn't been there.

Liz went upstairs feeling hopeful. There was still a chance that Ike would come over with her blazer and they could get back to where they were before Phil barged into her hospital room.

When she turned the TV to the news channel, another interview with Boris (Big Tiny) Tynkov was in progress. Apparently Big Tiny had gone through a second police interrogation this morning. He was visibly angry.

"How many times I got to tell the police I don't do kidnapping?" he asked the interviewer. "I got a wife and three girls. I wouldn't want nobody snatching them and I wouldn't snatch nobody else's women. What them two fellas done they done on their own. I didn't know nothin' about it."

The interview ended. The newscaster went on to comment that Tynkov's reputation would count against him. Too bad, Liz thought. Sure, Big Tiny was a loan shark who ordered his thugs to get rough with delinquent debtors, but he seemed sincere when he said he wasn't into kidnapping. What he'd said about his wife and daughters had touched a chord of sympathy. He shouldn't have to take the rap for something he didn't do.

If Ike knew she was feeling sorry for a notorious racketeer, he'd think the bump on her head had done more than erase part of her memory.

She spent the rest of the morning reviewing her notebook and adding to it. She hadn't written anything down since her kidnapping. Now, she recorded her reasons for thinking Kevin had planned it.

Kevin must have gotten his pot from another source. The skinhead wasn't a drug dealer; he was one of Big Tiny's collection thugs. Kevin must have been gambling. He lost a bundle and borrowed from Big Tiny's organization to pay it off, but he'd fallen behind. He was being threatened. He was desperate...

When she read what she'd written, another startling possibility hit her. What if Kevin had gone to his father, told him the predicament he was in and asked for the money? If his father got angry and refused, this could have been the motive for the murder. It all tied in with what she already knew—the argument Mariette overheard in the study and the anger Maybanks directed at Kevin during dinner.

Maybe Kevin went to the study later in the evening to try and get his father to change his mind. Maybe they argued. Maybe Kevin lost control and bashed his father's head in with the nearest object—the bronze bookend—still missing, even after police searched the apartment. But it had to be in the apartment. Kevin must have it well hidden.

He probably planned to sneak it out when he went back to school.

She recalled Dan saying Maybanks's wallet was empty. Kevin could have taken whatever was in it, but it wasn't nearly enough to cover what he owed Big Tiny.

He'd killed his father and cleaned out his wallet, but how was he going to raise the rest? He couldn't risk asking his mother for such a large sum of money. She might mention this to the cops when they questioned her, and they'd get suspicious. She also had a fortune in jewelry, but if he heisted any of it, the theft would be reported to the police. He couldn't take the chance. That's when he must have come up with the idea of having Emily kidnapped for ransom.

Her thoughts had gone beyond speculation. Now she felt certain that Kevin, the model son and loving brother, had murdered his father and set up his sister.

She knew if she'd figured this out, then Ike had, too. Her need to talk with him about it was almost painful.

A knock sounded at her door. Probably Rosa with a sandwich for her lunch, she thought.

"Rosa, you shouldn't keep spoiling me like this," she called, on her way to let her in.

When she opened the door, Ike was standing there with a big smile on his face. He had the Sohms Fifth Avenue bag under his arm and was carrying a large, flat box. She smelled the unmistakable aroma of pizza.

"Is it okay if *I* spoil you?" he asked.

Taken by surprise and flustered by the thought of

being kissed in the E.R., she could only say, "Come on in, Ike."

"It's lunchtime and I was in the vicinity," he replied, handing her the bag and the pizza box.

He didn't act like a man who'd stroked her hair and kissed her forehead and hand while she was out cold. Sophie must have exaggerated. "Does that mean you have to eat and run?" she asked.

"I can stay awhile. We have some catching up to do, Liz."

"We certainly do!" she said. She put the Sohms bag on a chair and carried the pizza box behind the kitchenette screen. She'd wait till they were settled with their lunch, then she'd tell him what she'd figured out.

"How are you feeling?" he asked, following her.

"Fine. I went to the doctor this morning."

"Everything okay?"

"Yes. Except I still can't remember anything about the kidnapping or the car crash. Shall I make coffee?"

"A Coke will be fine. Sorry your blackout's still with you."

"I'm not worried. I've had two doctors tell me it's only temporary."

They carried their pizza and drinks to the sofa.

"Before you begin to tell me what's been going on with the Maybanks case, there are some things I figured out for myself," she said.

"That doesn't surprise me."

"If that's supposed to be a compliment, I've heard better than that."

He cast her a grin. "I'm sure you have, my darlin' Colleen."

She stared at him. This remark could mean he was jealous, but he didn't look in the least jealous. "Is that why you haven't been in touch with me?" she asked.

"Right. I thought you'd be too busy."

"You should know I'm never too busy to talk about a current homicide case, especially one that's linked up with my kidnapping."

"So you figured there's a link," he said. "What else?"

She told him, adding, "I know you must have reached the same conclusions."

He nodded. "You're a great little sleuth, Liz. You're right on the nose. We think Kevin was into some kind of gambling and being threatened by Tynkov's loan sharks. When his old man refused to give him money to cover his losses, we believe they argued and Kevin lost control and killed his father. We think he planned the kidnapping after that and intercepted the ransom note when you were kidnapped by mistake. But, until we find the murder weapon with his fingerprints on it, we don't have enough evidence to charge him with murder."

"What about prints on his father's wallet?"

"Too smudged. He must have tried to wipe them off. But we're hoping he was in a hurry to hide the bookend and didn't take time to clean it off."

"Couldn't you charge him with planning the kidnapping, for starters?"

Ike shook his head. "It's out of our hands. The Feds have taken it over."

She sensed he wasn't pleased about this. "I guess that means they'll arrest Kevin soon and charge him with kidnapping," she said.

"Your guess is as good as mine," he replied.

"Well, getting back to the murder. Where do things stand now?"

"We figured Kevin would sneak the bookend from wherever he'd hidden it and dispose of it on his way back to school on Sunday. We planned to catch him at it and make an arrest, but it didn't happen."

"I know he didn't go back to school. I saw him this morning in Dr. Ray's office. He has the flu or something."

Ike looked surprised, and a bit disapproving. "You went to Dr. Ray's office?"

"Not to snoop. He's become my regular doctor. I went there so he could look at my head."

Now was the time to ask him about the secret she was sure had something to do with the murder. "Speaking of Dr. Ray—when you came to the hospital, you were going to tell me about your conversation with him, but we were interrupted," she said. "And weren't you going to tell me about Mrs. Maybanks saying something she didn't intend to?"

"Yes. I'll fill you in now." He took a swig of his Coke. "It was very difficult for us to seriously suspect Kevin. A nice kid, an honor student, very likeable, good relationship with his parents."

She nodded. "Not the sort of boy who'd do such horrible things."

"Gregory Maybanks turned antisocial after Vietnam," Ike went on. "But Ray and Schuler told me he came from a long line of distinguished professionals and solid citizens. And Maybanks himself had a reputation for honesty and integrity."

Liz grew impatient. *Why was he going on about Gregory Maybanks's background?*

"Schuler told me Mrs. Maybanks came from good people, too," Ike continued. "Her father was a carpenter—an honest, hardworking man, and her mother was a part-time nurse's aide. They scrimped to send Mrs. Maybanks to business school. She worked in Schuler's office for nine years. According to him, she was conscientious and trustworthy."

Liz's impatience began to rise. "If you're saying it seems impossible that a boy with all those good genes could do what Kevin did, I agree," she said. "But the fact remains, we both think he did. Now, will you please get on with what you were going to tell me?"

"Hold on to your Irish," Ike replied. "I gave you those backgrounds because they're part of the picture. Kevin didn't have any of those good genes. Mrs. Maybanks's accidental remark put me onto something I hadn't thought of. Both Kevin and Emily were adopted at birth."

SEVENTEEN

ADOPTED! LIZ WAS SPEECHLESS. This possibility had never entered her mind.

"It was a surprise for me, too," Ike said. "While I was talking with Mrs. Maybanks after the funeral, I said something about Emily being a pretty girl. That's when she made the remark that started me thinking. She said she knew Emily was going to be pretty from the first day they *got* her."

"Ooh, that sounds like an adoption, all right. Was she aware of what she'd said?"

"Apparently not. We continued talking about other subjects, but the remark stuck in my mind. I thought if Emily wasn't their natural child, Kevin might not be, either. I had a gut feeling I was on to something, but I didn't know what. That's when I decided to talk to Dr. Ray. I was sure he'd know if the kids were adopted, being the family physician and an old friend."

"Schuler would know, too, wouldn't he?"

"Right. I met with the two of them. They were very cooperative. They told me both kids were adopted. Dr. Ray set it up with the birth mothers and Schuler handled the legal part of it."

"At the time, did you think this had anything to do with the murder?" Liz asked.

"Like I said, I had a gut feeling."

"And was your gut right?"

He nodded. "They told me a strange story. You're not going to believe it. I didn't, at first."

This sounded intriguing, Liz thought. "Try me," she said.

Ike took a long drink of his Coke. "All right, here goes—Kevin's family background is about as bad as it gets. He comes from a long line of clever con artists, gamblers, convicted felons and even a murderer."

Liz couldn't believe what she'd heard. Ike must have seen the look of disbelief on her face.

"It's true," he said. "One of his grandfathers died in prison, while serving time for a swindle scheme that bilked hundreds of elderly people out of their life savings. The other grandfather did time for running an illegal gambling operation. One of his grandmothers operates a…well, let's just say it wasn't a Bible study class."

Startled as she was, Liz had to smile at this last item. Did he think she'd be shocked to hear the actual name for it? "What about his mother?" she asked.

"Very good-looking, according to Ray and Schuler. Smart, too, but the wrong kind of smart. She'd been in and out of jail several times on bunco charges."

"And his father?"

"A con man and a gambler. Never held a legitimate job in his life. Dr. Ray said he was shown pictures of him. He was handsome, but reported to have a violent temper. He'd been in jail off and on for assault and battery. At the time of Kevin's birth, he was in prison on manslaughter charges."

Liz thought this over for a few moments. "With genes like that, something was bound to come out. How could Kevin develop into such a charming young gentleman?"

"I never ran into a bunco artist who couldn't charm the birds off the trees. That's how they're able to swindle people."

"If Dr. Ray knew about this awful background, why did he allow the Maybankses to adopt the baby?" she asked.

"Here's the part you're not going to believe. Gregory Maybanks wanted to adopt a boy with the worst possible family background. He had Dr. Ray research the families of every boy baby up for adoption. Before Kevin came along, Maybanks rejected several boys because their backgrounds weren't bad enough."

Liz looked at him in disbelief. "You've got to be kidding."

"I'm not kidding, and you haven't heard it all yet."

"You mean Emily's background is bad, too?"

"More sad than bad. When the Maybankses were looking for another baby to adopt, Gregory specified that he wanted a girl from respectable but low IQ parents. Emily's mother was only fifteen when Emily was born. She'd never made it into high school and never had a job. The father was eighteen, a high school drop-out, but at least he worked steadily, digging for a septic tank company."

"Were they married?"

"Yes, but the marriage was on the rocks. They were going to split up and neither of them wanted the baby."

Thousands of couples adopt babies from average backgrounds and they turn out great, Liz thought. Why did Maybanks deliberately want one kid with a criminal family background and another whose mother and father were short on brains? He must have known he was asking for trouble, especially with Kevin, who was loaded with bad genes.

She was about to bring this up for discussion, when the phone rang. It was Sophie, wanting to know how she was feeling.

"I'm fine. I went to the doctor this morning."

"Have you thought anymore about what I told you?" Sophie asked.

"Ike's here. He dropped by with pizza. We're talking about the Maybanks case," Liz replied.

Sophie got the message. "Oops. Sorry I interrupted. I'll call you later."

When Liz hung up, she noticed Ike looking at her with an indefinable expression on his face. "Was that Sophie?" he asked.

"Yes." She had a pretty good idea what was on his mind. He knew Sophie had witnessed the tender scene in the E.R. and he also knew Sophie wouldn't keep something like that from her best friend.

"Well, let's get on with our talk," he said. "When I

heard about Kevin's background, he became my number one suspect."

He'd brushed off the unspoken subject. She felt a pang of disappointment. Evidently he didn't want to discuss the E.R. moment. Maybe he wished it had never happened. Well, if that's the way he wanted it, she could pretend she hadn't given it a second thought.

"All you need now is to catch Kevin with the bookend," she said. "Too bad he got sick on the day he was supposed to drive back to school. You could have him under arrest right now."

"Finding the murder weapon in his possession might not be enough," Ike said. "Sure, it's strong evidence, but, like finding traces of blood and hair in the cat carrier, it's circumstantial. Kevin would clean the bookend before packing it in his luggage. His prints wouldn't be on it. The lab would pick up traces of blood, but a clever attorney could make it seem as if someone had planted it."

Liz pictured Kevin at his hearing, charming the judge with his handsome, clean-cut appearance and disarming manner. "But what if he's caught trying to dispose of it?" she asked.

"A clever attorney could also make it seem as if Kevin panicked when he found the bookend someone else had stashed in his car, and tried to get rid of it so he wouldn't be blamed for his father's murder."

"Will Schuler be his lawyer?"

"Schuler doesn't handle criminal cases, but you can

bet Kevin will have the best defense attorney money can buy."

"If catching him with the bookend doesn't nail him, what would?"

"If he hid the bookend in a hurry, without cleaning it, and if we could find it before he removes it from its hiding place, his prints and his father's blood would be on it. That should be enough."

"Could Kevin have sneaked the bookend out, already, and stashed it in his car? I know you said he's been under surveillance ever since the murder, but…"

Ike shook his head. "His car has already been searched. The bookend is in the apartment somewhere."

"You're sure there's no way it could have been taken out?"

"Positive. But for a while we went along with the cat carrier slant. We considered Emily of course, but as an alternate angle, we thought the killer could have stashed the bookend in the cat carrier and Emily took the cat to Mariette's place without noticing the bookend was in there. Mariette might have caught sight of the bookend when they took the cat out. It was in the back of the carrier, so she wouldn't have noticed the blood. She didn't ask Emily why it was there. Emily was terribly upset. Mariette probably decided not to upset her further by questioning her."

"I get it," Liz said. "Later in the evening Mariette could have caught a news report of the murder mentioning that a bookend was the murder weapon but Emily didn't hear the report."

"Right. We thought Mariette could have decided Emily did it. She's very fond of Emily, so to protect her she got rid of the bookend."

"Then, without telling Emily she'd heard about the murder, she brought her home. Most likely she thought Emily was in shock about killing her father. It all made sense."

"Yeah, we thought we'd find the bookend with the killer's prints on it, in or near Mariette's apartment. Nothing turned up in the apartment. A search was made of trash bins within a wide radius of Mariette's place. The collection was made Friday morning, so the bookend would have turned up quick, but it didn't. Besides that, when we questioned Mariette we were convinced we were on the wrong track, and the bookend never left the apartment."

Liz gave a sigh. "This is the strangest case I've ever followed. I don't understand why Maybanks would deliberately adopt babies with undesirable backgrounds. Why would he take the risk when he could adopt kids with normal parents and grandparents?"

"That's another part of this bizarre story," Ike said. "Maybanks was trying to prove something. Ray and Schuler explained it. They said while they were in college, Maybanks got interested in the theory of an eighteenth-century philosopher and author. Some French guy. They said this guy believed that all babies are born good, and with the potential to achieve, and that environment and environment alone shaped a child's character and intelligence."

Liz got the connection. "So, if all babies are born good, Maybanks figured a baby from a long line of criminals could grow up to be an exemplary character if he were raised in the best possible environment, and a baby from low IQ parents could develop high intelligence."

"That's it, exactly. Raise a kid from infancy in a home with intelligent adoptive parents. Provide him with cultural and spiritual advantages and the best education money could buy, and surround him with luxuries and privileges. Then it wouldn't matter what he came from."

Liz shook her head. "Sounds to me like Maybanks forgot about providing the most important thing of all—love."

"Right," Ike said. "He equated love with money and material things. But from what I noticed, Mrs. Maybanks gave Emily plenty of real love. She couldn't do the same for Kevin, though. Maybanks monopolized Kevin. He took full charge of his son's development and left his daughter's upbringing strictly to his wife."

"When did Maybanks get interested in the French philosopher's idea?"

"According to Ray and Schuler, it was during a Philosophy course in their senior year at Princeton, but it wasn't till he got back from Vietnam that he started talking about it seriously. Then he got married. He was unable to father children because of his war injury, so he and his wife decided to adopt. That's when he told

Dr. Ray he intended to put the philosopher's theory into practice."

Everything she'd heard while eavesdropping outside Gregory Maybanks's study came rushing back to Liz's mind, starting with Schuler's question. *"So, you think the boy did it, Con?"* and ending with the remark she'd thought about, over and over, since that day— the remark which epitomized the rationale of Gregory Maybanks's murder! *"Setting himself up for ultimate doom."*

"They suspected, from the first, that Kevin was guilty, didn't they?" she asked.

Ike nodded. "And if Kevin goes to trial and his background is admissible, they're ready to testify."

"I wonder why it took so long for Kevin's bad genes to show up?"

"I'm no shrink, but I think it happened when he heard his father say 'no' for the first time. All his life the kid always got what he wanted. Having his father deny him the money and get angry with him shocked those bad genes right out in the open."

A shrink would say the same thing, only in different words, Liz thought.

"Did Mrs. Maybanks know her husband was trying to prove this philosopher was right?" she asked.

"According to Ray and Schuler, she knew, but she didn't believe in it herself."

"I'm surprised someone as intelligent as Maybanks would go along with a crackpot idea like that."

"Many intelligent people were taken in by it. Evidently this French guy had quite a following at one time. His environment theory stayed around through the nineteenth century and even into the early part of the twentieth. Maybanks was influenced by it, well into the genealogical era."

"It sounds crazy. Wouldn't it be ironic if Maybanks had a few nuts on his own family tree?"

Ike laughed, then cast her a questioning smile. "Are we pretty well caught up on the case now?"

She returned the smile. "Yes. Thanks. I know, now, that finding the bookend before Kevin cleans it up is more important than anything else. I feel as if you've told me more than you should have."

"The D.A.'s okay with it. He knows you've been helpful in the past."

"I haven't been much help on this one."

"It's not over yet." He glanced at his watch. "Liz, I have to leave in a few minutes. Can we change the subject?"

"Sure. To what?"

"To us." She saw a smile in his eyes. "I guess you didn't realize there was an *us.*"

She caught her breath. She didn't know how to reply.

"I didn't realize it, either, until that night in the E.R.," he said. "When I saw you lying there, all smashed up and unconscious, it struck me, what if you didn't come out of it?" He took her hands in his. "Liz, I knew right then what we have is a hell of a lot more than a close friendship."

Where were all the words she wanted to say? She

could only look into his eyes and nod her head. There was no need for words, anyway. A moment later, she felt his arms around her.

"Yes, there certainly is an *us,*" she whispered when the kiss ended.

EIGHTEEN

SHE FELT AS IF her entire life changed in those few minutes. Now, as she listened to the sound of Ike's footsteps going down the stairs, his parting words echoed in her mind, "I'll come over tonight around six. I'll bring a bottle of wine and some takeout. How about Mexican?"

In those few, innocuous words, she heard the essence of the change in their relationship. No need for her to ask if he'd like to come over tonight. No need for him to ask if she'd like to have dinner with him. They both knew they wanted to see each other again, as soon as possible.

The words reflected Ike's thoughtful nature, too. He knew she wouldn't feel like going out for dinner or cooking a meal.

She felt happy and comfortable and so right.

She sat down with her notebook to record what Ike had told her. It filled several pages. The strange behavior of Gregory Maybanks seemed even more incredible when she saw it written down. She wondered if Kevin knew anything about his family background. Probably not. She had a hunch neither he nor Emily had ever been told they were adopted. That would tie right in with Gregory Maybanks's offbeat ideas.

Rosa came up to see how she was feeling.

"I went out to the store and when I came back Joe told me your cop friend was here earlier," she said.

"Yes, he brought pizza for lunch." Rosa gave her a sharp look and a knowing smile. Liz felt as if she had *Liz and Ike* and a big, red heart tattooed on her purple forehead.

"I was going to ask you to eat with us tonight, but maybe you have other plans," Rosa said.

"Yes, he's coming back later." The Moscarettis would know what time Ike arrived and what time he left, she thought. Well, it looked as if Ike's visits were going to become so frequent that Rosa and Joe would stop keeping score. The thought made her smile.

She turned on the TV news channel—not that she expected there'd be anything new about the Maybanks case. With Kevin's trip back to school postponed, the investigation had come to a standstill.

She pictured him recuperating from the virus, or whatever it was he had. He'd be making plans to get the bookend out of its hiding place, cleaning the blood and his fingerprints off, and putting it in his luggage. Where could he have hidden it? It was small enough to be tucked out of sight almost anywhere, but the police had searched the apartment twice without finding it. Time was running out. Ike might have to settle for nabbing Kevin with a clean bookend and risk a clever attorney building a frame-up.

A clever attorney would put Kevin on the stand at his trial, she decided. The charming deceiver might con the jury into believing he'd, indeed, been framed. Kevin could be acquitted. She felt greatly disturbed by this possibility.

When, a moment later, viewers were advised to stand by for a late-breaking bulletin, she felt no surge of anticipation. All she could think of was Kevin charming his way out of a murder rap. If only some indisputable evidence would turn up—something that would convince the jurors Kevin hadn't been framed.

She tried to concentrate on what the newscaster was saying. "Racketeer Boris 'Big Tiny' Tynkov was arrested an hour ago on kidnapping charges. Tynkov, who allegedly masterminded the abduction of a retired NYPD detective's daughter, denied any involvement. He is being held without bail, pending an as yet unscheduled hearing."

The newscaster went on to say the arrest had been made after the FBI took over the NYPD investigation of the case.

Liz was stunned. Again, she felt the racketeer was being unjustly accused because of his past criminal activities, none of them kidnapping.

Her belief that Kevin was guilty of both the murder and the kidnapping was so strong in her mind that it seemed as if the news media should have picked up on it. But her kidnapping and Gregory Maybanks's murder were separate cases. Ike and Lou might be keeping their suspicions about Kevin's possible involvement in the kidnapping under wraps. For the time being, they wanted Kevin to think he'd gotten away with murder and kidnapping, too.

With suspicions about Kevin being kept quiet so as not to tip him off, it looked as if the FBI agents hadn't been informed of a possible link between Kevin and the kidnapping. But there might be an additional reason. She remembered Pop telling her that when the FBI came in on a NYPD case, the cooperation sometimes wasn't one hundred percent. Some agents acted superior, Pop said. And in this case, the arrest of Boris Tynkov made it look as if the FBI had stepped in and solved it after the NYPD failed.

She finished writing in her notebook. When she put the notebook in her purse, she noticed the Sohms Fifth Avenue bag on the chair. Her blazer had gone from Gregory Maybanks's study to Kevin's clothes closet, and then into the bag which had been dropped on the street, retrieved by the doorman and eventually ended up in Ike's hands. It must be a mass of wrinkles by now, but at least the bag would have protected it from attracting a layer of dust and lint.

She wouldn't be wearing it again until fall, anyway, she thought, taking it out of the bag. She'd have it cleaned and pressed and put it away until the weather turned cool.

As she expected, the blazer was wrinkled. Otherwise it looked okay, she thought, scanning the dark blue wool fabric. But something on the right sleeve caught her eye. A few flecks of…what? Not lint or dust, but some sort of grainy grayish stuff.

Had her blazer fallen off the chair in Gregory Maybanks's study and picked up something on the floor? Her first instinct was to brush it off. But curiosity stopped her. She decided to take another look at the grainy stuff and see what it was. Close scrutiny didn't tell her anything. Now she was *really* curious. She had a magnifying glass somewhere. After a search through drawers and cabinets, she found it.

A few moments later she stared in puzzlement at the magnified grayish flecks on the sleeve of her blazer. There wasn't enough of the stuff to identify it right away, but maybe if she thought about it awhile, she'd come up with something.

Her experience following homicides kicked in. If this stuff had been on the floor of the study, maybe it had something to do with the murder. She dismissed this idea. Officers would have found the substance while going over the crime scene. But she couldn't rid her mind of the notion that this unidentifiable stuff might somehow be linked to the murder.

She looked at the mysterious substance through the magnifier again. Had she ever seen anything like it before? *Think...*

Now it struck her. She remembered Gram using stuff that looked like this when her old cat, Hercules, was still around. This gray substance had to be cat litter!

Instantly, her mind started racing. Bruna had hung her blazer in Kevin's closet, thinking it was his. There wasn't anything that dark blue fabric didn't attract. If it had been hung next to the jacket Kevin had on the night of the murder and his jacket had cat litter on it...

In a flash, she knew where Kevin had hidden the bookend. It was in one of the big bags of cat litter she'd seen in Emily's cabinet.

She recalled seeing two bags on the shelf. One had been opened and the top folded down. It looked half-full. The other was still sealed. Kevin must have carefully opened it, stashed the bookend in it and resealed it. The officers who searched Emily's room might have looked in the open bag, but when they saw the other bag was sealed, they didn't bother with it. Pop would call this sloppy police work. He'd be tickled when she told him she'd uncovered the indisputable evidence she'd hoped would turn up.

She was on a roll now. As quickly as questions came, she had the answers. Kevin had transferred some of the litter from the full bag into the open bag to make room for the bookend. That's how he got cat litter on his sleeve. Then, when her magnetic blue blazer was hung next to it, some of the cat litter had been transferred.

As Pop had suggested, before hiding the bookend in the litterbag, Kevin first put it in the cat carrier, then changed his mind. That would account for the blood and hair on the cushion.

She remembered Bruna saying Emily had gone to her mother's bedroom after the argument with her father. While she was with her mother, Kevin had gone to his father's study to try and persuade him to change his mind about giving him the money. The second refusal had enraged him. After he'd killed his father, he'd rushed toward his own room with the bookend, trying to decide what to do with it. On the way, he'd heard his mother and Emily talking in his mother's room. Knowing Emily was not in her room, he got the idea of stashing the bookend somewhere in there until he could smuggle it out to his car. That had to be how it was.

She recalled how willing he was to have the police search his room. Why wouldn't he be willing? The bookend was hidden in Emily's room.

She put the blazer back into the bag. How could she wait until Ike came over to tell him all this? He wouldn't be here for at least three more hours. She decided to phone the station house, and see if he was there. She'd tell him she'd figured out something very important concerning the bookend. If that didn't bring him here on the double, nothing would.

Ike wasn't there. Neither was Lou. The reception clerk asked her if she wanted to speak to another detective. She asked for Sid Rothman. "Tell him it's Liz Rooney," she said. Sid was an old friend of Pop's. He knew about her interest in following homicides and he also knew she'd helped Ike solve previous cases. She'd tell him she had important information for Ike.

Sid came on. "How are you, Lizzie?" he asked. "We heard what happened to you, of course. Your father stopped at the station house while you were in the hospital and told us you were going to be all right."

"I'm doing fine, Sid. I have a favor to ask of you."

"Sure, Lizzie. What can I do for you?"

She asked him if he could take a message for Ike. "I have some extremely important information for him, Sid."

"I'll see that he gets your message the minute he comes in," Sid promised. He paused. "You sure gave us a shock with that kidnapping, Lizzie. You're like family. You being Frank Rooney's daughter, everyone on the squad wanted to get in on it, so the Lieutenant made it a house investigation. Then the FBI stepped in. I guess you heard there's been an arrest."

"Yes. Boris Tynkov. But I don't believe he had anything to do with it."

"The two men who died in the crash were members of his organization."

"But Big Tiny insists they did it on their own. He says kidnapping's something he'd never do."

"Yeah, I know, and it's true he's never been involved in anything like that, but his record and the two kidnappers being part of his organization, that was enough for the FBI."

With his little dig at the FBI, Sid didn't sound anymore convinced than she was that Big Tiny had planned her kidnapping, Liz thought, after they said goodbye.

While waiting for Ike to contact her, she decided to spruce herself up a bit. She knew she'd looked terrible when he was here before, but she'd been taken by surprise. Now, she applied some makeup to her forehead. It helped. At least her hair looked okay. She'd washed it this morning and arranged it so it hid part of her forehead. Red hair didn't go well with purple, though.

But now with her camouflage, she was pleased with the effect. She put on a dash of lipstick. Not bad. She changed into white pants and a green silk shirt, and was trying to decide whether to go all out and wear the jade earrings Gram had given her, when the phone rang. It was Ike.

"Sid gave me your message. What's up?"

"Are you in the squad room?"

"No. I just left there. I'm in my car, on my way over to your place. This better be important. I left a stack of reports on my desk."

As if she'd tell Sid it was important if it wasn't. "If you decide it's not important after I tell you, you can go back to your blasted reports," she said.

"Whoa. Don't get your Irish up. I'll be there in ten minutes."

He was. When she opened the door he gave a whistle. "Look at you! What happened?"

This was his way of telling her he liked what he saw. "I thought you'd seen enough of the redheaded monster," she said.

Instead of replying, he caught her up in his arms and kissed her. "Now, what's this big, important information?" he asked.

She took his hand and led him to the sofa, saying, "You'd better sit down for this."

He sat down. "So let's have it."

"I figured out where the bookend is hidden."

He looked pleasantly startled. "I know you wouldn't

say something like that without being damn sure of it," he said. "Tell me what you figured out."

She told him.

"Let's see your blazer," he said.

She took it out of the bag.

He examined the sleeve, put the blazer back in the bag, and got to his feet. "I'll have to give you a rain check on our Mexican dinner," he said. "And I'm taking the blazer with me."

She understood. He was going straight to the May-bankses' apartment. "I hope you find it," she said, though she had no doubt the bookend was exactly where she'd figured it would be.

He paused at the door, saying, "I know I'll find it. You did it again, Liz."

With that he was gone, without so much as a light kiss or a small hug. But she couldn't feel anything except satisfaction. She'd helped solve another case, and she'd seen much more than a kiss in his eyes.

NINETEEN

HOURS LATER, WHEN SHE was in bed, asleep, Ike phoned. She was groggy when she picked up, but the sound of his voice brought her fully awake and alert with anticipation.

"I found the bookend, right where you said it'd be," he said. "I guess I woke you up but I was sure you'd want to know. Go back to sleep. I'll call you tomorrow."

"How could I go back to sleep now? Can't you fill me in?"

"All right. Kevin's prints were on the bookend. He's under arrest. He's still sick, so he's in bed under police guard."

Liz pictured Kevin charming the officers on guard, making them think if he actually did bash his father with the bookend, there had to be a good reason for it. *Even with this indisputable evidence, would he do the same with a jury?*

"After confronting Kevin with the evidence, we had him call Schuler and waited till he got there with a defense attorney before we took his statement," Ike said. "He stated he told his father that he wanted to turn in his Corvette and buy a Porsche like one a friend at school had. The Porsche cost more than he'd get for the

Corvette, so he asked for money for the balance, he said. Then he said his father got very angry and refused to give him the money, saying he should be satisfied with his Corvette."

Clever strategy, Liz thought. By telling the police he wanted money for a new car, Kevin had side-stepped any questioning which might have brought his gambling losses to light. She was sure Kevin lied when he said he asked his father for money for another car. The amount after the trade-in wouldn't have been unreasonable. His father would have given it to him. But Kevin needed a very large sum of money. He had to tell his father he'd been gambling.

"I think that car story was a lie," she said. "I think Kevin admitted to his father that he was being threatened by loan sharks. He was confident his father would hand over the money. His father had never refused him anything in his entire life."

Ike gave his approval. "You're right on the mark. Gregory Maybanks wouldn't have gotten angry about Kevin wanting to trade in his Corvette. What set him off was the realization that Kevin was a gambler, like his natural father."

"And that the environment theory was a fallacy."

"Right. That would have angered him. According to Kevin, he flew into a rage. Kevin admitted hitting his father with the bookend when his father made a threatening remark and opened his desk drawer. Kevin ended his statement by saying he thought his father was going to come at him with some sort of weapon."

Liz could see it all in her mind. The deadly clash between a father enraged by bitter disillusionment and a son denied something for the first time in his life.

"I think he made that up about thinking his father had a weapon," she said.

"Sure he did," Ike replied. "The cops didn't find anything in the desk drawer that could have been used as a weapon. But I can smell a self-defense plea."

A frightened son. An out-of-control father. Liz sighed, picturing a sympathetic jury. But would a jury be sympathetic if it could be proved that Kevin had set his sister up for abduction? "Are you still working on Kevin's involvement in the kidnapping?" she asked.

"Not since the FBI took over and arrested Tynkov. Lou and I told the Feds what we suspect, but with the two kidnappers being part of Tynkov's organization, apparently they believe this outweighs our suspicions."

"Well, I guess you've told me enough for now. Thanks for filling me in."

"I'll phone you, tomorrow, as soon as I can. And by the way, did I tell you you're incredible?"

HER MIND WAS TOO ACTIVE for sleep to take over. She lay awake for quite a while. Was it possible that the FBI would dismiss the idea of Kevin planning the kidnapping? There was no real evidence that he had anything to do with it. His involvement in it existed only in her mind and in the minds of Ike and his partner, Lou Sanchez.

On second thought, this might not be true. Surely

Big Tiny knew who owed his organization big bucks. He could have put two and two together. All he had to do was open his mouth. Why hadn't he done this? After some thought, she believed she knew. Loan sharking was the mainstay of a racket that had made Big Tiny a multimillionaire. Maybe he didn't want to risk losing it. Even if he got sent up for a long term, with his power, he could still operate from prison.

Boris "Big Tiny" Tynkov was an example of the dregs of human society. She could never condone what he did to make his millions, but that didn't justify his being sent away from his family, while a punk rich kid got off scot-free.

She felt herself growing drowsy. Drifting into a pre-sleep languor, she thought about Ike and their changed relationship. There hadn't been any expressions of endearment, yet, but Ike had come close with his final words on the phone tonight. *"By the way, did I tell you you're incredible?"*

She fell asleep with a smile.

SHE WOKE IN THE MORNING with a strong sense of having the troublesome angles of the case sorted out. Sure, Kevin and his attorney might convince a jury that he'd killed his father in self defense, and Kevin wouldn't get the long sentence he deserved. He might even be acquitted. But the kidnapping would be a separate charge. If Kevin thought he was home free now that Big Tiny had been charged with the kidnapping, he was mistaken. He wouldn't get away with it. She'd see to that.

She'd state how she was shoved into the kidnap car outside the Maybankses' apartment building. She'd describe the high-speed car chase and the argument between the two kidnappers, with the driver saying he thought they'd snatched the wrong girl, and the other one insisting they hadn't, and mentioning "the kid" and the red-haired sister. She'd quote him saying he and the driver would be dead meat if Big Tiny found out they'd kidnapped someone.

Then it struck her. *Her memory had come back!*

Her first instinct was to call Ike. But it was only half-past-six. He wouldn't be at the station house this early and she didn't want to call him at home and wake him up. She knew he'd been working late last night.

She decided to call him after she'd showered and dressed and had her morning coffee.

At seven o'clock, she turned on the TV. While she drank her coffee, she'd find out if Kevin's arrest had made the morning news. She pictured him in his own bed, surrounded by all the comforts he'd always known, confident that he'd only get a short sentence, if any, for killing his father in self-defense, and believing he'd never be charged with planning the kidnapping.

But now she had her memory back. The sooner she let the proper authorities know the truth, the sooner Big Tiny would be released from jail. And the sooner Kevin would be charged with the kidnapping.

A bulletin came on about Kevin's arrest for the murder of his father. A photo of Kevin was shown. It looked like a school yearbook photo. A reporter must have gotten it from Kevin's school. Liz noticed Kevin was wearing a tweed jacket. It might be the same jacket he was wearing the night he bludgeoned his father to death and then hid the murder weapon in the bag of cat litter. Clever as he was, he didn't realize some fabrics picked up residue like a magnet picked up nails.

She reached for the phone and called Ike's home number.

"What's up, Liz?" he asked, when he heard her voice.

"My memory's back," she replied. "What I remember will get Boris Tynkov off the hook and hang Kevin on."

"Great. The timing's perfect," he said. "Tynkov's hearing is set for this morning. I'll notify the D.A. that you have a statement. But remember, this hearing is strictly about Tynkov—not Kevin. I'll pick you up in an hour."

POP HAD TAKEN HER to a couple of hearings, but never to one where the charge was kidnapping, or where she'd make a statement for the accused.

After she and Ike sat down, she glanced at Boris Tynkov, seated in the first row with his attorney. She saw him turn around and smile at the woman and the three teenaged girls sitting behind him. His wife and daughters, Liz decided. Mrs. Tynkov, who reminded Liz somewhat of Bruna, was dabbing at her eyes with a tissue. The girls looked subdued and sad as they talked quietly among themselves.

Liz got the distinct feeling that this was a close family.

She hoped that her statement would change things for them.

The judge listened to her tell about her terrifying experience and the conversation she'd heard between her two captors. That conversation was something she'd never forget. She related it without hesitation and hoped it would convince the judge that, although Tynkov's men had carried out the kidnapping, it had been planned by someone other than Big Tiny.

She also hoped the talk between the hairless goon and the driver would implicate Kevin. If the part where Hairless said she had to be the right girl because the kid described his sister as red-haired, didn't work, the part where he said he'd seen her coming out of the church after her father's funeral might.

Mindful of Ike's warning, she'd been very careful not to mention Kevin's name, but the judge and the D.A. would have to be pretty dense not to realize the intended victim was Emily Maybanks. The wheels had been set in motion.

When she was finished, her instincts told her she'd convinced the judge that Boris Tynkov had nothing to do with the kidnapping. She was right. The judge absolved Big Tiny of the charges and told him he was free to go.

When she and Ike were on their way out, she glanced over her shoulder and watched the Tynkov family happily embracing one another. For an instant, she forgot what this loving husband and father did to provide a life of luxury for himself and his wife and daughters.

Ike noticed the glance and smiled. "I have to admit I'm pleased with the way this turned out. You did a great job, Liz. Kevin's a clever kid, but I don't see how he can wriggle out of this one."

"I hope he's watching TV when this news breaks," Liz said. She wished she could see the expression on Kevin's face when he realized her memory of the kidnapping was restored, and he hadn't gotten away with the kidnapping, after all.

"I have some paperwork to do at the station house," Ike said as they got into his car. "But after that I have the rest of the day off. I'll drop you at your place and come over later. Would you like to go out for lunch, or shall I pick up something?"

"Takeout sandwiches would be great," she said.

"Good," he replied. "And we'll go out for dinner tonight."

This was settling into something very comfortable, she thought.

THE NEWS OF BIG TINY'S release came on TV soon after she got home. By this afternoon the story might break about Kevin's involvement in the kidnapping. This would be a double-header. She'd helped solve the murder and the kidnapping, too. She and Ike would have plenty to talk about.

She wondered how Mrs. Maybanks would react to this new charge against her son. And how would Emily take the news that the brother who'd always seemed so loving and protective had planned to have her kidnapped?

The phone rang. It was Dan. She'd had so much on her mind, she'd forgotten to call and tell him she'd be back at work tomorrow. Also, she hadn't let him know her memory was restored. But he'd understand. He knew when she was following a case, it took over her mind.

"Forgive me for not checking in with you," she said. "I'll be at work tomorrow without my blackout. I woke up this morning remembering everything."

"You're forgiven," he said. "I know you got your memory back. I heard you made a statement at Tynkov's hearing and he was released. And from what you picked up from the kidnappers, it looks like Kevin Maybanks planned the whole thing. Do you believe he's capable of that, Lizzie?"

"Yes. I've suspected it for quite a while."

"If *you* believe he could do such a thing, then he did," Dan said with a laugh. "I'll see you tomorrow, Lizzie."

A few minutes later the phone rang again. This time it was Sophie. At first Liz thought she'd caught the news about Big Tiny and about Kevin, and wanted to discuss it. But Sophie only wanted to take up where they'd left off.

"Did Ike say anything about the E.R.?" she asked.

Liz decided to give Sophie more than she expected. "No, but we've gone beyond the E.R.," she said.

Sophie gave a delighted squeal. "Oh, I wish we could

talk, but I'm on a coffee break and I have to get back to the car. I'll call you tonight."

Liz couldn't resist saying, "Not tonight."

"Ooh," Sophie said. "Tomorrow, then."

A little later, Ike arrived with barbecued beef sandwiches and a six-pack of beer.

"There should be a news bulletin soon," he said as they settled themselves on the sofa to watch TV and eat. Liz liked having him there beside her, with both of them knowing their feelings had deepened. She couldn't decide if the barbecued sandwiches were the best she'd ever tasted or if the general atmosphere made it seem that way.

When they finished eating, he took one last pull on his beer and looked her squarely in the eyes. "We have some catching up to do, and I'm not talking about murder or kidnapping cases," he said.

"Then what *are* you talking about?" she asked, even though she was sure she knew.

"This." He drew her close. They kissed. They kissed again.

"We've had too many delays and interruptions," he said.

Just as he spoke, a TV newscaster announced a bulletin. They both turned to look at the screen.

"Hold that thought till this is over," Liz said.

He cast her a grin. "I'll hold your hand till it's over, too."

The newscaster read the bulletin. "Eighteen-year-old Kevin Maybanks, son of slain real estate magnate

Gregory Maybanks, already arrested for killing his father, now faces an additional charge for planning a kidnapping which left two men dead and the kidnap victim injured and suffering from amnesia."

He continued with details, saying the victim's memory had been restored and she'd given a statement at Boris Tynkov's hearing, resulting in Tynkov's release.

"One hour ago, FBI agents formally accused Maybanks of the second crime. Maybanks, confined to his bed with a respiratory infection, remains under guard in his home," the newscaster said.

By the time the newscaster finished reading the bulletin, more information had come in. After Kevin's arrest for the murder, investigative reporters had been delving into Kevin's activities dating back several years. They'd discovered that Kevin was an inveterate gambler. His cell phone and his computer at school made it easy for him to play the horses regularly at every track from Saratoga to Santa Anita. They also found out that he'd recently suffered heavy losses.

"There goes his *money for a Porsche* statement," Ike said.

"Despite mounting evidence that the need to cover gambling losses was the motive for both the murder and the kidnapping, Maybanks's attorney, present during the arrest, had no direct comment, but said a statement would be forthcoming after he conferred with his client," the newscaster said. He urged viewers to stay tuned.

"Mounting evidence—that includes my statement at the hearing," Liz said. "Will my memory loss be used to discredit my statement? What if the defense brings this up at Kevin's trial and makes it seem as if my memory wasn't accurate?"

She'd barely spoken when the newscaster announced that Mrs. Maybanks and Emily had both made statements to the FBI, describing how Kevin had urged Emily to go out for a walk on the evening of the abduction.

"That'll do it," Ike said. "But I wasn't worried. You've already convinced a judge with what you heard. You'd convince a jury, too." He'd been holding her hand. Now he gave it a pat, saying, "You're very convincing, Liz Rooney. You convinced me to disregard a couple of things I had my doubts about."

"Like what?"

"Well, for one, your age."

Was he saying he thought she was too young for him? She'd set him straight. "I'm twenty-three," she said. "Last I heard, that's well into adulthood."

"I'm pushing thirty, Liz."

"So what? When I'm sixty, you'll be sixty-six."

He laughed. "Didn't I just say you already convinced me the age difference doesn't matter?"

"And how did I do that, oh ancient one?"

"With your sharp mind, mostly. But your looks probably had something to do with it, too. Even your red hair."

"*Even* my red hair?"

"Right. I'd always heard red-headed people had tempers to match."

"So that's the other thing you had your doubts about.

You didn't want to get involved with a red-headed Irish vixen."

"Right, again. But after you were a red-headed vixen a couple of times, I found out it wasn't so bad. Blow off steam and then it's over. That's better than having a woman sulk and not tell you what's bugging her."

"I promise never to sulk," she said. "I'll always tell you what's bugging me."

They were in a middle of a kiss when the voice of a TV newscaster intruded, announcing a forthcoming bulletin. It had to be something about Kevin, Liz thought. By this time his attorney might have prepared a statement.

"Another interruption," Ike muttered. But she noticed he was just as interested in the bulletin as she.

A few moments later they looked at one another in surprise. Kevin's attorney had issued a startling announcement to the news media. Kevin would plead guilty to planning his sister's kidnapping.

TWENTY

"How could Kevin's attorney let this happen?" Liz asked.

"He's going for a plea bargain," Ike replied. "Kevin pleads guilty to the kidnapping charge, the city is spared the expense of an additional jury trial, and Kevin gets a lighter sentence."

"I never heard of an attorney making an announcement like that on TV."

"He's probably got something up his sleeve."

Ike was right. The newscaster was continuing with an item even more electrifying. Kevin's attorney had released Kevin's taped confession of guilt in the kidnapping to all radio and TV news programs, with instructions that it be aired as soon as possible.

Before they could comment on this most unusual move, the tape came on. Kevin began to speak.

"My name is Kevin Maybanks," he said, his voice sounding strong for someone too ill to get out of bed, and also accused of two major crimes.

"I am making this statement of my own free will," Kevin continued. "I planned the kidnapping of my sister because I was driven to desperation. I owed forty thousand dollars to Boris Tynkov's loan sharking organization and when I asked my father to help me out, he not only turned me down, but he became so enraged I was sure he was going to attack me, physically. I deeply regret accidentally killing my father in self-defense, but I feared for my life."

He was presenting himself as a victim, Liz thought. Did he really believe this would cancel out the fact that he'd planned to victimize his sister?

Kevin went on to say a Tynkov collection agent he knew only as Sergei the Scalp had issued an ultimatum. Pay up or start shopping for a wheelchair.

He said he couldn't think of any way to raise the money until he got the idea of having Emily kidnapped for ransom. His mother had more money than she knew what to do with, he said. He made the kidnappers promise to be gentle with Emily. She'd be returned, unharmed, and he'd be spared bodily injury. Nobody would be hurt.

Liz shook her head as she listened to the flawed reasoning. He sounded as if he actually believed the kidnapping was justified. This kid needed psychiatric help.

At first, Sergei the Scalp wouldn't go for the kidnapping plan, Kevin stated. He said he struck a private deal with Sergei. Offered plenty of money and assured that Big Tiny would never find out how he'd managed to collect from Kevin, Sergei finally agreed to get a trusted cohort to help him kidnap Emily.

The ransom would be one hundred thousand dollars. When the ransom was paid, Big Tiny would get his forty grand and Sergei and his aide de camp would split the remainder. It was too tempting an offer to turn down.

"With all that money, they planned to break away from Big Tiny and go someplace where they'd never be found," Kevin said.

The plan was simple. Kevin described Emily to Sergei and set the time and place for the kidnapping. He knew his mother would be frantic when Emily disappeared. She'd get the ransom note the day after the snatch and gladly pay up, according to instructions, keeping the police out of it. Emily would be released. Sergei the Scalp would wipe out Kevin's gambling debt, then head for parts unknown with his cohort and the loot.

Kevin said he realized the plan had gone awry when Emily didn't disappear. When he learned about the car crash, he watched for the mail, intercepted the ransom note and destroyed it. He ended his statement by saying he never meant for anyone to get hurt, and again said he was driven by desperation.

"Excusable homicide and desperation," Ike said. "That attorney's damn clever. But a brother setting his sister up for kidnapping—that's going to be a hard nut to crack."

"I just thought of something," Liz said. "Kevin still owes Tynkov the forty thousand."

Ike laughed. "After his close call today, you can bet Big Tiny isn't going to look for any more trouble. Forty grand is peanuts to him. He'll just write it off and be thankful he didn't have to take the rap."

"Kevin identified him by name as a loan shark. Won't that get Big Tiny into legal trouble?"

"Tynkov has been hauled into court more times than I can count. Tax evasion, fraud, extortion, among other things. But his slick attorneys always got him off. If you hadn't made your statement, this kidnapping charge would have been the only one to stick."

"But won't Big Tiny order his thugs to go after Kevin? They could get to him, even if Kevin's in prison."

"Possibly. Unless he decides it would be smart to forget the whole thing."

The voice of the newscaster again drew their attention.

Mrs. Maybanks had made a statement to the media. She'd said that she and Emily had stood by Kevin after he was accused of killing his father. They would have forgiven him for that, she said, but planning to have his sister kidnapped was something neither she nor Emily could forgive. Emily was heartsick, she said. She did not think either of them would want to have anything to do with him ever again.

"Sounds like the kid might spend the rest of his life without the love and support of his mother and sister," Ike said.

"Do you suppose Dr. Ray and Mr. Schuler will show him any support, like visiting him?"

"I think they will. They both feel some responsibility for what happened."

The phone rang. It was Joe Moscaretti, and he

sounded agitated. "Liz, some men just came into the building. They insist on seeing you."

"And you don't want to let them up?"

"Not unless your cop friend is still there. I wasn't sure if he left."

"He's still here, Joe. You can tell the men to come up."

Ike looked at her in puzzlement. "What was that all about?"

"Apparently Joe doesn't like the looks of some men who are here to see me."

Just as she spoke, they heard the tramp of feet on the stairs.

"I'll get the door," Ike said. He didn't wait for a knock. Liz caught sight of four men in the hallway. She knew why Joe was reluctant to let them up. They looked like a collection of mobsters left over from a Grade-B crime movie.

Ike stood in the doorway, blocking it, asking, "What can I do for you?"

A large man in the forefront looked past him and saw Liz. "I come to see the lady," he said.

She was startled when she recognized Boris Tynkov.

Ike must have recognized him at the same moment. He stepped aside and motioned for the men to come in. Liz noticed one of them was carrying a large box.

Big Tiny fixed his eyes on Liz. "You done me a favor today," he said. "I come to show thanks."

He snapped his fingers. The man with the box stepped forward and placed the box at Liz's feet.

"Some bread and cakes my wife bake special," Tynkov said. "And I put in what else I hope you like. You see when you open box." He turned toward the door. "You enjoy in health."

His three henchmen moved ahead of him, opening the door, scanning the hallway before signaling the okay.

On his way out, Tynkov halted, turned around and looked at Liz. "You ever got trouble, you ever need something, I want you should let me know," he said. "Big Tiny never forgets." With that he and his men lumbered down the stairs.

Liz and Ike looked at each other and burst out laughing.

"Let's see what kind of goodies a racketeer's wife whips up," Liz said.

They opened the box. Nestled among an assortment of cellophane-wrapped cakes, cookies and breads, were six bottles of champagne.

"Big Tiny has excellent taste in wines," Ike said, scanning the labels.

"And Mrs. T knows how to bake cookies," Liz replied, biting into one. "It was sweet of him to come here himself instead of having this delivered, wasn't it?"

"Yeah, he's a sweet guy, all right."

"You better be nice to me," she teased. "You heard what he said."

"I heard. The first fight we have you'll go running to Big Tiny. Next, you'll be consorting with the Russian Mafia."

"Oh, that would be exciting. Do you think I'd have my own bodyguard?"

He brought her into his arms. They shared their best kiss yet.

"You already have a bodyguard," he said.

* * * * *

REQUEST YOUR FREE BOOKS!

2 FREE NOVELS
PLUS 2 FREE GIFTS!

WORLDWIDE LIBRARY®

Your Partner in Crime

YES! Please send me 2 FREE novels from the Worldwide Library® series and my 2 FREE gifts (gifts are worth about $10). After receiving them, if I don't wish to receive any more books, I can return the shipping statement marked "cancel." If I don't cancel, I will receive 4 brand-new novels every month and be billed just $5.24 per book in the U.S. or $6.24 per book in Canada. That's a saving of at least 34% off the cover price. It's quite a bargain! Shipping and handling is just 50¢ per book in the U.S. and 75¢ per book in Canada.* I understand that accepting the 2 free books and gifts places me under no obligation to buy anything. I can always return a shipment and cancel at any time. Even if I never buy another book, the two free books and gifts are mine to keep forever.

414/424 WDN FEJ3

Name   (PLEASE PRINT)

Address   Apt. #

City   State/Prov.   Zip/Postal Code

Signature (if under 18, a parent or guardian must sign)

Mail to the **Reader Service:**
IN U.S.A.: P.O. Box 1867, Buffalo, NY 14240-1867
IN CANADA: P.O. Box 609, Fort Erie, Ontario L2A 5X3

Not valid for current subscribers to the Worldwide Library series.

Want to try two free books from another line?
Call 1-800-873-8635 or visit www.ReaderService.com.

* Terms and prices subject to change without notice. Prices do not include applicable taxes. Sales tax applicable in N.Y. Canadian residents will be charged applicable taxes. Offer not valid in Quebec. This offer is limited to one order per household. All orders subject to credit approval. Credit or debit balances in a customer's account(s) may be offset by any other outstanding balance owed by or to the customer. Please allow 4 to 6 weeks for delivery. Offer available while quantities last.

Your Privacy—The Reader Service is committed to protecting your privacy. Our Privacy Policy is available online at www.ReaderService.com or upon request from the Reader Service.

We make a portion of our mailing list available to reputable third parties that offer products we believe may interest you. If you prefer that we not exchange your name with third parties, or if you wish to clarify or modify your communication preferences, please visit us at www.ReaderService.com/consumerschoice or write to us at Reader Service Preference Service, P.O. Box 9062, Buffalo, NY 14269. Include your complete name and address.

WWL11B